The Canterbury Bridge Tales

David Silver & Tim Bourke

Master Point Press • Toronto, Canada

Master Point Press, 331 Douglas Ave.
Toronto, Ontario, Canada M5M 1H2
(416)781-0351 Email: info@masterpointpress.com
Websites: www.masterpointpress.com | www.teachbridge.com
www.bridgeblogging.com | www.ebooksbridge.com

Library and Archives Canada Cataloguing in Publication

Silver, David, 1934-, author
       The Canterbury bridge tales / David Silver & Tim Bourke.
Short stories.
Issued in print and electronic formats.

ISBN 978-1-77140-019-0 (paperback).--ISBN 978-1-55494-611-2 (pdf).--ISBN 978-1-55494-656-3 (epub).--ISBN 978-1-77140-805-9 (mobi)
       1. Contract bridge--Fiction. I. Bourke, Tim, author II. Title.

PS8587.I272C36 2015   C813'.54   C2015-903687-9
                                               C2015-903688-7

Canada |•| We acknowledge the financial support of the Government of Canada.
       Nous reconnaissons l'appui financier du gouvernement du Canada.

Editor	Ray Lee
Copyediting	Steph VanderMeulen
Interior format	Sally Sparrow
Cover design	Olena S. Sullivan/New Mediatrix

1 2 3 4 5 6 7   18 17 16 15
PRINTED IN CANADA

For Amara, Emilia, Emmett and Shane

CONTENTS

PROLOGUE

March, with its gray skies and rain, had banished wintry February and bathed at least a few days in chilly sunshine, through which beckoned the Spring Nationals bridge tournament — a little later than usual this year. The bridge community was making its triannual pilgrimage to distant cities. This time, they were traveling from the far corners of North America to Canterbury, Florida, seeking masterpoints of every hue — platinum, gold, silver, even gray and pink.

It is a long drive from Toronto to Canterbury, and there were many of us on the road in the days before the tournament was due to start. My partner and I checked into a hotel in Walterboro, South Carolina, aiming to continue on our pilgrimage to Florida the next day. Perhaps I should not have been surprised, as I relaxed in the lobby that evening with the latest edition of USA Today, to see a succession of others arrive at the same hotel — all clearly bridge folk with the same destination in mind. It was natural for us all to gather in the lounge, fall into conversation, tell stories of Nationals past and imminent, and of course share a hand or two.

My first conversation that evening was with a fellow I knew slightly and recognized as a fellow Canadian. He was a Bronze Life Master, a man who was perhaps the most ethical player I have ever met. From the time he first picked up a bridge hand, he played the game with a kind of chivalry, believing in truth, honor, and courtesy. His opponents respected him as a gentle yet skillful foe. He had come from Handsover, Ontario, to compete at the Nationals despite the distressing news that Bruce Gowdy would also be there.

"Although there's not much point in playing if Bruce is going to be there," he commented. "You're competing for second place."

"But I heard Bruce had given up tournaments and was running a duplicate game in a retirement home?" I responded.

"He had," he replied, "but last fall he announced that he would be re-enlisting in the bridge wars. Everyone was quite surprised."

"What happened?"

"Well, it all started at his birthday party…"

"That sounds intriguing — tell me more."

And his tale began.

1

THE BRONZE LIFE MASTER'S TALE

When Mr. Bruce Gowdy of Handsover, Ontario, announced that he would shortly be celebrating his eleventy-first birthday with a party of special magnificence, there was much talk and excitement in the Handsover Bridge Club.

Bruce was very famous and very peculiar, and had been the wonder of the club for more than ninety years, since becoming the youngest player ever to win the Spingold. The trophies he had brought back from his travels had become a local legend, and it was popularly believed, whatever the veteran bridge players might say, that his apartment in Handsover was filled with souvenirs of his many victories in North America and Europe. And if that were not enough for fame, there was also his prolonged vigor to marvel at. Time wore on, but it seemed to have little effect on Mr. Gowdy. At ninety he was much the same as at fifty. At ninety-nine they began to call him "well-preserved," but "unchanged" would have been nearer the mark. There were some who shook their heads and thought this was too much of a good thing; it seemed unfair that anyone should possess (apparently) perpetual middle age as well as (reputedly) inexhaustible bridge skills.

Bruce remained on visiting terms with his family and he had many devoted admirers among bridge players, but he had no close friends until some of his younger relatives were older. The eldest of these, and Bruce's favorite, was young Peter Hambly. When Bruce was ninety-nine, he decided to become Peter's mentor and began teaching him the secrets of the Bridge Masters. Bruce and Peter happened to have the same birthday, September 22.

"You had better come and live with me, Peter, my boy," said Bruce one day, "and then we can play bridge every day and celebrate our birthdays together." At that time, Peter was still in his tweens, as the bridge players called the inept twenties, the years between childhood and automatically becoming a Life Master at age thirty-three.

Twelve more years passed. Each year, the local bridge players had given Peter and Bruce lively combined birthday parties at the club, but now something quite exceptional was being planned for that autumn. Bruce was going to be eleventy-one (111), a rather curious number and a very respectable age for a bridge expert (Oswald Jacoby himself had reached only 130), and Peter was going to be thirty-three, an important milestone for a bridge player.

The party naturally involved a duplicate game, and during the course of the evening, I watched the pair negotiate the following hand.

Dealer West. NS vul.

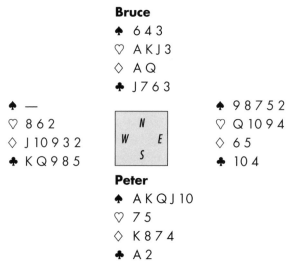

Bruce
♠ 6 4 3
♡ A K J 3
♢ A Q
♣ J 7 6 3

♠ —
♡ 8 6 2
♢ J 10 9 3 2
♣ K Q 9 8 5

♠ 9 8 7 5 2
♡ Q 10 9 4
♢ 6 5
♣ 10 4

Peter
♠ A K Q J 10
♡ 7 5
♢ K 8 7 4
♣ A 2

West	Bruce	East	Peter
pass	1NT	pass	2♡*
2NT	pass	pass	dbl
3♣	dbl	pass	4♣
pass	4◇	pass	4NT*
pass	5♡*	pass	6♠
all pass			

West, who was not a particularly skilled player, felt the need to be active and so he tried a kamikaze unusual notrump overcall. (Terence Reese, who counseled against giving away information in the auction when you are unlikely to buy the hand) would not have approved. And in this case, for certain, he would have been right.

Peter received the opening lead of the ◇J. He won this trick in dummy with the queen and drew all five rounds of trumps, throwing hearts from dummy. He had noted that East had failed to give preference after the 2NT overcall — obviously, he wanted West to suffer through playing the hand. Peter had also seen two heart discards from West so far.

After he cashed the ♡A, to which West followed, Peter concluded that West had begun with 0=3=5=5 shape. These cards remained...

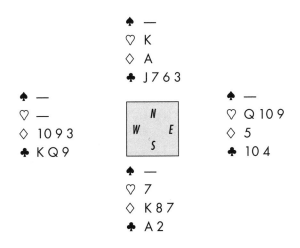

...and Peter claimed, citing a criss-cross squeeze on West.

Challenged by the opponents, he explained. "I know West has kept 3-3 in the minors and I'm going to play the ♡K next. If he discards a diamond, I cash the ♢Q and cross to hand with the ♣A to cash the ♢K and ♢8. A club is no better a choice, for then I can play ace and another club. West wins the ♣K but then dummy is high."

The opponents conceded and Bruce smiled affectionately. "Well done, nephew!" he roared. "Now you are ready for the Nationals."

The next morning they climbed into Bruce's Studebaker and set off. I happened to meet up with them later, just as they arrived at the tournament.

"Uncle Bruce, I don't understand why we're going on a cruise ship," complained Peter. "I thought the Nationals were being played in a convention center!"

"Peter, you must learn to listen when grownups speak to you. The hotels are sold out for the entire ten days, so the ACBL is putting us on this ship and running some extra tournament sections here. Yes, there's an upcharge of a thousand dollars per player, but what's a couple of grand, more or less, when you're attending a national tournament?"

"Well, let's get settled in at least — ah, here comes a director now." Peter flagged down a passing official. "Excuse me, I'm sorry to bother you, but we've lost our way."

"Where do you want to go?"

"Our cabins, of course."

"Cabins?"

"Yes, where we sleep."

"The elevator to the forward berths is right over there. You want Deck 2."

"Thank you. Uncle Bruce, I was right, this is the way."

"Good! They've probably put our luggage in the cabin already. I must say I'm tired."

"Do you wonder? After that long drive down from Ontario?"

"No, Peter, I suppose I don't. But we'll have a great tournament now, though, won't we?"

"For sure. I have to say, though, Uncle Bruce, I still don't see how we can be playing in the Nationals if we're in the middle of the Caribbean."

"Technology, my boy, technology. You know how we punch our pair number into that little black box before every round? Well, our results are posted into a database that will compare them to the other scores in our section and rank us all, wherever we're playing. That's how you can see a percentage immediately, which shows how we fared against the field. Not your mother's duplicate game, eh, Peter?"

Having no playing commitments of my own until the next day, I followed to see what their cabin looked like. As they made their way forward, a tall man in a suit and tie waylaid them.

"Are you planning to play the Open Pairs, gentlemen?" he asked.

"Why, yes — when does the first session start?"

"In about a quarter of an hour, more or less. You need to get seated."

"We haven't bought an entry yet. How do we know which table to sit at?"

"Choose one. It doesn't matter. Just type your pair number and direction into that little machine on the table. Make sure your opponents do the same before you play any hands."

"Our opponents?"

"They'll be along right away. The room is starting to fill up, the game will start shortly. When the round is over, the machine will display the number of the table you are to proceed to next. Everybody moves, North-South and East-West."

"I guess we'll figure it out." Peter turned to Bruce. "We can find the cabin later — time to play bridge."

"All right. I'll just find a washroom and be right back."

Peter had no sooner found a vacant table and sat down when a pleasant-looking middle-aged couple walked over. I thought they looked vaguely familiar but couldn't place them.

"Good afternoon! May we join you? I'm Charlie and this is Helen."

"Please sit down. My partner will be back in just a moment. I'm Peter."

"Pleased to meet you. Whom are you playing with?"

"Bruce Gowdy — do you know him?"

"Oh yes. You should have a drink, you'll need it. Steward!"

"Yes, sir?"

"Coffee for me and the lady, scotch on the rocks for my young friend here."

"Certainly, sir."

The drinks and Bruce arrived, as did a caddy with boards. I had no plans to play in this event, so I pulled up a chair behind Peter.

"Bruce, these folks are Charlie and Helen."

"I think we may have met before — good afternoon. Into the booze already, Peter?"

The director announced that they could start play, and the competition commenced. The second board saw Charlie bid an aggressive slam:

Dealer East; E-W vul.

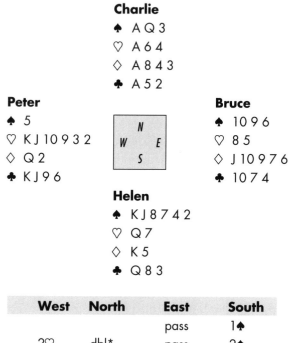

Charlie
- ♠ A Q 3
- ♡ A 6 4
- ◇ A 8 4 3
- ♣ A 5 2

Peter
- ♠ 5
- ♡ K J 10 9 3 2
- ◇ Q 2
- ♣ K J 9 6

Bruce
- ♠ 10 9 6
- ♡ 8 5
- ◇ J 10 9 7 6
- ♣ 10 7 4

Helen
- ♠ K J 8 7 4 2
- ♡ Q 7
- ◇ K 5
- ♣ Q 8 3

West	North	East	South
		pass	1♠
2♡	dbl*	pass	2♠
pass	6♠	all pass	

With four unattractive suits to choose from, Peter opted to start with his singleton trump. Helen surveyed her prospects. She won the first trick with the ♠A, cashed the spade queen, and continued with two top diamonds and a diamond ruff in hand. When Peter showed out on this trick, any hope of a three-suit squeeze vanished. The best chance now was a Belladonna strip-squeeze in the pointed suits, which would require West to have begun with 1=6=2=4 shape and to hold the ♣K plus at least two of ♣J, ♣10, and ♣9.

Helen played another round of trumps to reach this position:

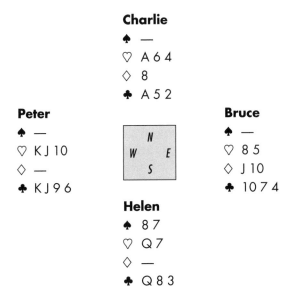

Charlie
♠ —
♡ A 6 4
♢ 8
♣ A 5 2

Peter
♠ —
♡ K J 10
♢ —
♣ K J 9 6

Bruce
♠ —
♡ 8 5
♢ J 10
♣ 10 7 4

Helen
♠ 8 7
♡ Q 7
♢ —
♣ Q 8 3

On the next trump, if Peter threw a low club, the last trump would indeed signal his doom: he would be thrown in via whatever suit he discarded from, to lead away from his king in the remaining suit. So he discarded the ♣9 and played the ♣J on the final spade — a valiant effort, but not good enough. Helen simply led a club. Seeing the end-play coming, Peter rose with the king, but Helen won with the ace and finessed the ♣8 on the way back, losing only a heart trick at the end.

Bruce was impressed. "Now I'm sure I've met you before — who are you exactly?"

"Ask Charlie," replied Helen, smiling, as she moved for the next round.

The rest of the session proceeded similarly, with the opponents playing double-dummy, while Peter and Bruce had a pajama game, alternate tops and bottoms. There was a break between sessions and they retired to the smoking room for much-needed respite. I tagged along for lack of anything better to do.

"Who is that gorgeous blonde?" Peter asked of no one in particular. Bruce turned and looked about.

"That's Freya, a European client — quite talented," he answered. "She's playing a lot with a young pro named Gavin and doing quite well lately."

They watched as Freya asked the steward about the location of her cabin.

"Your cabin?" he asked.

"Yes! Where we sleep. I'm afraid I must sound awfully stupid, but we usually fly and I've never been on a ship before."

"You're not the only one," said the steward, smiling. "You'll find all the berths forward, right down there."

"Thank you very much. Gavin, come along, I was quite right, this is the way."

Peter noticed her companion for the first time. He looked to be about thirty and was wearing a suit and tie. He appeared bemused.

"Sorry, I was looking at the sea. What did you say?"

"The cabins are that way."

"Oh, good! Let's hope our luggage is there already."

His eye caught Bruce and Peter.

"Well, if it isn't Bruce Gowdy. Didn't expect to see you here."

"I decided to come and show young Peter here what a Nationals is like. Good to see you again, Gavin."

"Very confusing these ships, aren't they? Did you find your cabin yet?"

"We know where it is, just haven't had time to get down there yet. Did you play board sixteen today?"

"Yes, we defended four hearts."

"Did you beat it?

"No, it was brilliantly played by someone named Sami. Look at the hand record."

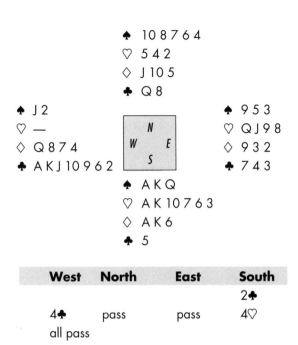

	♠ 108764		
	♡ 542		
	◇ J 10 5		
	♣ Q 8		

♠ J 2   ♠ 9 5 3
♡ —   ♡ Q J 9 8
◇ Q 8 7 4   ◇ 9 3 2
♣ A K J 10 9 6 2   ♣ 7 4 3

	♠ A K Q		
	♡ A K 10 7 6 3		
	◇ A K 6		
	♣ 5		

West	North	East	South
			2♣
4♣	pass	pass	4♡
all pass			

"I led the ace and king of clubs, declarer ruffing with the six of hearts. He cashed the ace of hearts and three top spades, followed by playing ace, king, and another diamond to leave me on lead."

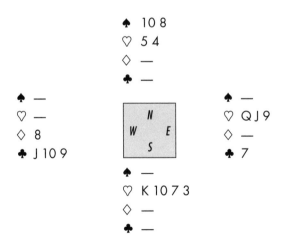

	♠ 10 8		
	♡ 5 4		
	◇ —		
	♣ —		

♠ —   ♠ —
♡ —   ♡ Q J 9
◇ 8   ◇ —
♣ J 10 9   ♣ 7

	♠ —		
	♡ K 10 7 3		
	◇ —		
	♣ —		

"I exited with a diamond, ruffed in dummy with the four of hearts, and Freya played the jack of hearts. Declarer underruffed with the seven.

Freya's club exit was ruffed with declarer's three of hearts and over-ruffed in dummy with the five of hearts. A spade lead couped Freya's ♡Q9. Four hearts bid and made."

"Not at our table," said Bruce condescendingly. "At Trick 2 Peter shifted to a spade. Consequently, declarer couldn't shorten his trump holding by ruffing a club and there was no coup available in the end-game."

"Of course. Now why didn't I spot that? You know, I think I banged my head on something on the way down here — I guess I'm a little more dazed than I thought."

"Give me your hand," said Freya. "Let's head to the cabin."

They went off together, and a moment later a slight young man entered, cheerful and smiling.

"Good afternoon, steward," said the man.

"Good afternoon, sir."

"This is the smoking room, I suppose?"

"Yes, sir, and the bar."

"And how long before we sail?"

"About a quarter of an hour, sir, more or less."

"Could I get a coffee?"

"Certainly, sir."

"Excellent! I need it. As a matter of fact, steward, you'll probably see a lot of me during this tournament. Yes, you'll get to know me quite well, so I thought I'd warn you to begin with."

"The warning is an honor, sir."

The newcomer looked expansively round the room, taking us in with the rest of it. "Wow, that must have been a rough night, because I can't remember anything about it now. But never mind, it's a gorgeous day, anyway."

"It is, sir," the steward agreed, pouring coffee. "A pity some people should be alive to spoil it."

"What's that?"

"I was talking to myself, sir."

"So, how many passengers have we got?"

"Not many, sir. It's our slack time of year."

An elderly woman bustled in, smartly dressed in jeans and a sweater, carrying an armful of magazines.

"Darren Spielman! I thought I knew that voice!" she exclaimed.

"Mrs. Rivermore!" The coffee drinker rose to greet her. "What a surprise. How are you? What are you doing here?"

"Playing some bridge, of course," she replied. "But I'm afraid we're in for a very dull trip. There's nobody on board — at least nobody who is anybody. Though, of course, the poor creatures can't help that."

"We'll try and cheer each other up then, Mrs. Rivermore. Maybe we can even play a side game one evening. By the way, at which port are you disembarking?"

"Yes, all friends at sea, of course. I can't recall where I'm getting off but I'm sure someone will tell me when we get there. By the way, when I said there was nobody on board … between you and me, there is one person on board to whom I take a strong exception. He's a rabbi. Clergymen at sea are dreadfully unlucky. We shall probably all go to the bottom."

Darren smiled. "Well, if we do I'll blame the rabbi entirely. In my opinion, they have no right to let clergymen travel at all. Rabbis ought to stay at home in their synagogues and do good, and not go roaming about all over the world putting other people's lives in danger."

"Well, the best thing we can do is ignore him," said Mrs. Rivermore. "Nicely, of course, but firmly."

"Just as you like. But will we save the ship by doing it?" Darren mused.

"Oh, that's funny!" She smiled.

Darren looked up as an older, bearded gentleman came in.

"Look. Speak of the—"

"Hi. Sol Bristow," the gentleman introduced himself. "Do you know where I can get some notepaper and an envelope?"

Darren ignored him, saying in a loud voice to Mrs. Rivermore, "And your husband, how is he? Still playing bridge, I hope."

"Dear Benjamin, I regret to say, passed away last year playing in the Vanderbilt."

Darren made a gesture of regret.

"Yes," continued Mrs. Rivermore, "I should have been there with him but somehow I was never able to get away. The penalty of popularity. My good friend Mabel, the leading masterpoint holder in Collingwood — you don't know her, of course — she was saying to me at the club only the other day—"

"Good afternoon," the man who called himself Sol tried again.

This time, Mrs. Rivermore pointedly turned away. "How odd, the people one meets in public places. Never mind. Let me see, where was I?"

"With your great friend Mabel, whom I don't know."

"Oh yes, of course. And then that strange man whom neither of us knows interrupted. Never mind. Mabel pointed out to me very clearly that I was in danger of neglecting my duty. She said to me quite plainly, almost brutally — and she can be very brutal sometimes — 'My dear Genevieve,' she said, 'you must remember you are a daughter of a Gold Life Master, an expert's daughter — an expert's wife. Your place is sponsoring a team in the Spingold. In fact, she was so insistent on my leaving town that if I didn't know her really well, I would have felt she wanted to get rid of me. Still, I have taken her advice; I have abandoned Toronto's gaieties and come to help some impoverished bridge pros."

"I'm awfully sorry to bother you, madam, but could you tell me the date?" Sol tried again.

"What was that?"

"I ought to know, of course, seeing that it's the date we sail, but my memory's so—"

"You're trying to start a conversation with me, aren't you?" accused Mrs. Rivermore.

"Well, frankly, as we're all shipmates, the sooner we get to know each other the better, don't you think?"

"That, sir, is a matter of opinion."

"Oh, I'm very sorry, if — I thought we could perhaps be informal, on board ship."

"Possibly in the days of Ely Culbertson. Not having been there myself at that time, I can't say for certain. But under the circumstances, I can't possibly give you the date."

"Fine. I'll find it out for myself." Thoroughly disgruntled, the rabbi headed off in the direction of the steward.

"Do you think I was clear enough, Darren?" she asked, turning back to him.

Darren mumbled non-committedly, then looked up. "Was that a siren I just heard? We must be sailing shortly."

"Then I shall go on deck and wave farewell to the dear old sandy beaches," declared his companion. "I'm told that in many parts of Florida they're disappearing. Still, there's no place like it, especially in the winter."

"That's what all the bridge players say," Darren said, smiling.

Mrs. Rivermore paused. "What does the weather matter to a bridge player? They rarely go outside. Well, I'll see you later."

"I suppose so." Darren sighed.

Bruce and Peter had been listening to these exchanges somewhat bemused, and now looked slightly guilty, as eavesdroppers might.

"Well," said Bruce heartily, "I'm afraid we must get back to the tournament."

"Yes, me too," said Darren. "I should go and register, I guess."

Back on the tournament deck, Bruce and Peter greeted the new opponents who had arrived at their table. I took my chair behind Peter once more.

"Good afternoon. I'm Harold and my partner is Waldemar," said the elder of the two gentlemen. Peter did not react to this announcement; Bruce looked briefly puzzled but soon became engrossed in the cards in front of him.

The first board was a flat part-score, but the third was quite interesting. East-West were vulnerable and Waldemar, sitting East, was the dealer. He started the bidding with a pass, and a spirited auction ensued.

Bruce
- ♠ A K 2
- ♡ 6 4
- ◇ 9 6
- ♣ A K Q J 7 6

Harold
- ♠ Q J 10 9 6
- ♡ A Q 10 9 2
- ◇ 8
- ♣ 9 2

```
        N
    W       E
        S
```

Waldemar
- ♠ 8 7 3
- ♡ J 8 7 3
- ◇ J 10 7 5
- ♣ 8 3

Peter
- ♠ 5 4
- ♡ K 5
- ◇ A K Q 4 3 2
- ♣ 10 5 4

West	North	East	South
		pass	1◇
2◇[1]	3♣	pass	3◇
pass	3♠[2]	pass	3NT
pass	4NT	pass	6NT
all pass			

1. 5-5 in the majors.
2. Spade values.

West made the obvious lead of the ♠Q, which Peter won in dummy. He then cashed six club tricks, discarding a spade and two hearts from his hand. But when West showed out on the second diamond lead, Peter showed his hand and conceded one down.

"I can't make it with a 4-1 diamond split," said Peter.

Waldemar harrumphed. "Oh, I wouldn't say that."

"Well, I certainly don't see how it can be made," said Peter. "Please tell me."

"Win the opening lead with the king of spades. Then play five rounds of clubs to reach this position:

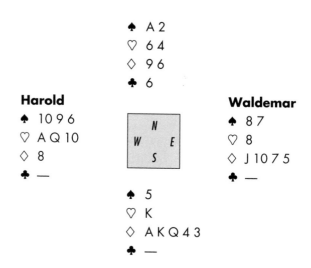

♠ A 2
♥ 6 4
♦ 9 6
♣ 6

Harold
♠ 10 9 6
♥ A Q 10
♦ 8
♣ —

Waldemar
♠ 8 7
♥ 8
♦ J 10 7 5
♣ —

♠ 5
♥ K
♦ A K Q 4 3
♣ —

"By now you know West started with 5=5=1=2 shape including the ♥A, and East had 3=4=4=2 distribution. When you play the last club, East has a number of unpleasant choices.

"If East parts with a spade, you throw a diamond, then play the ♦AKQ, reducing everyone to three cards — which means that West has to reduce to a singleton in one of the majors. If it is a heart, then dummy parts with a spade, and playing a heart sets up the six of hearts for the twelfth trick. If West reduces to a singleton spade, then the ace and two of spades are declarer's eleventh and twelfth tricks.

"Obviously, if East discards a heart, throwing a diamond is hopeless, so you discard the king of hearts. Now comes the clever bit — you must lead the nine of diamonds and duck East's ten or jack — you need East to have begun with ♦J10. You win the spade return and cash your four diamond tricks."

During the second smoke break, Bruce, Peter, and I returned to the bar to find Darren and the rabbi in earnest conversation.

"Has it struck you by any chance that there is something odd about this boat?" asked Darren, turning and appealing to Gowdy.

"No, it hasn't," Bruce replied. "Just a bridge game like any other."

"It has me. I think there's something very odd about this ship."

"I don't follow you," chimed in Peter.

"Well," said Darren, "don't you find it odd that none of us can remember the date — or where we're supposed to be going? And I've noticed lots of other little things. For instance, there aren't that many bridge players, and without them, the ship would be practically empty."

"If you take my advice, you'll get some fresh air on deck," commented the rabbi.

Just then Freya arrived, taking advantage of the smoke break to stretch her legs. Darren turned to her.

"Do you mind if I ask you a question?"

"Of course not," said Freya. "I hope it's not a bridge question?"

"Do you know where you are going to?"

"Of course I know where I'm going."

"On this ship I mean."

"Certainly."

"Thank goodness!" exclaimed Darren. "Now I *am* going to get some fresh air!"

Gavin bundled in, almost bowling over Darren in the doorway. "Why did you rush off like that, Freya?" he asked. "That guy was just being stupid. You would have to be peeking to defend the hand that way."

"Or be a really expert bridge player."

"It's beyond double-dummy."

"Sorry, I'm a bit nervous," admitted Freya

"You've no need to be now — we've set sail."

"Have we?"

"Yes. I saw the water moving by the porthole."

"You're right. Why, we're well out, almost in open water. You know, a man just now asked me if I knew where I was going. I said I did."

"Of course you do."

"Funny question, though, wasn't it? You don't think he—"

"Of course, not," Gavin assured her. "None of these people can possibly know."

"What makes you say that?"

"I can't quite remember, Freya, but—but—"

"Yes?"

"Haven't you and I done something really bad?"

"Like what?"

"I don't know. But if we had, Freya, could they separate us? Where could I find another partner who can play bridge the Silver way?"

"We've done nothing that isn't right," said Freya firmly.

"I don't know, it seems to me this thing — if there is something — that we've done is big, and yet that it's only something to do with the car."

"Our car?"

"Yes. I think I forgot … to turn off the engine."

"You silly man, of course you did. We — agreed — that. That's what we agreed."

"There's nothing very wrong in not turning off the engine. And yet — Freya, you're quite certain there isn't something else?"

"There's nothing else, I'm certain."

Gavin looked out of the porthole at the ocean sliding by. "I wish I could remember how we got here."

"Let's go out onto the deck."

Again, Freya encountered Darren in the doorway; he stepped aside to let them pass before entering the bar. He had a strange look on his face as he walked up to the steward.

"I'm right, aren't I?" he asked.

"Right, sir? Right in the head, do you mean?"

"You know what I mean."

"No, I don't sir. Right about what?"

"You — I — all of us on the ship."

"What about all of us on this ship, sir?"

Darren paused, as if thinking about how to phrase his answer. "We are — now answer me truthfully — we are all dead, aren't we?"

The steward seemed not in the least put out by such an odd query and answered matter-of-factly. "Oh yes, sir, we are dead. Quite dead. Except for some of the bridge players, and they are short-haul passengers. But the rest don't usually find out as soon as you have, as a rule."

"And how long have you been … you know?"

"Me, sir? Oh, I was lost young."

"I don't understand."

"No, sir, you wouldn't, not yet. But you'll get to know lots of things as the voyage goes on."

Darren thought about it. "Tell me one thing," he said, leaning forward.

"Anything I can, sir."

"Where — where are we sailing to?"

"Heaven, sir."

"Heaven?" said Darren, taken aback.

"And Hell, too; it's the same place, you see."

"But…" As Darren was absorbing this, Mrs. Rivermore breezed back in. He straightened up and addressed the room.

"Listen to me, everyone," he said, raising his voice slightly.

"I beg your pardon?" said Mrs. Rivermore.

"What's the matter now," said the rabbi.

"Every one of us — all of us on this boat — we're done for," announced Darren. "Well, maybe not you three," he allowed, looking at Bruce and Peter and me.

"I knew we should have thrown Mr. Bristow overboard," said Mrs. Rivermore, not altogether in jest.

"I mean it. You needn't believe me if you don't want to. It's true all the same. We're dead people."

"Oh, go away and sleep it off," replied Bristow.

"I'm sober enough. And the ship's not sinking. I don't mean that, either. Come here. Feel my pulse. There is a line drawn on the floor and I'll walk it if you want me to. Now, look at me closely — I am sober, aren't I?"

"Yes, I think so."

"The last time I heard a bridge player say 'Yes, I think so' was when he was asked if he was the best player in the room. Now, you admit I'm sober. You'll have to take my word for it that I'm not mad.

"I began to suspect this afternoon after lunch. Nobody seemed to know where they were going. I'd forgotten myself, though I didn't want to admit it. When I was quite convinced, I got drunk. That was only natural. All my life I've faced facts by getting drunk. Well, when I woke up again, about an hour ago, you were all in the bar. I went all over the ship. Into the officers' quarters and everything. No one said a word to me for a very simple reason: there's no one on board. No captain, no crew, no nothing."

"If there's no crew on board this ship, Mr. Spielman, may I ask who waited on me at lunch?" retorted Mrs. Rivermore.

"There's no one at all on board this ship! Excepting the bridge people and the steward. He waited on you at lunch. He's in charge of the ship."

Bristow had heard enough. "Really, Darren, I think that—"

"That I don't what I am talking about? Very well, then, answer me this. Who have you seen on board this ship since she sailed? Except ourselves and the bridge players? Have any of you met anybody else? A sailor, an officer of any sort, even a tour guide? Well, speak up."

"Well, I must have met someone, of course."

"You should have met someone, you mean. But you haven't. And where are you disembarking?"

"Disembarking? I'm going to — I'm going to — mind your own business."

"Come on, where are you landing?"

"I'm taking a little holiday, that's all. I'm going first to — to—"

"You see, you can't remember. I'm right! I knew I was."

"What about the bridge players?" asked Mrs. Rivermore, staring meaningfully at Bruce and Peter. "There are dozens of them and I've played in a side game and even chatted to some of my opponents."

"I think that the tournament is not really here on this ship. It is actually happening somewhere else; we enter it just for a while, play a little bridge, and then return when we leave the hall. And there is something very odd about the opponents — not sure what yet, but I will figure that out too, eventually. Still, can you really, honestly tell me you've seen nothing strange about the ship?"

"Nothing whatever, excepting you. And I've been on dozens of cruises," Mrs. Rivermore said, sniffing.

"Well, I'll tell you one little thing I noticed about her that struck me as slightly different," said Darren. "This ship doesn't carry a port light, and she doesn't carry a starboard one either! Now is she the same as any other ship? Now can you settle down to your cards?"

"You are mad!" It was Gavin. He and Freya had come in from the deck and were standing in the doorway bemused, listening to this bizarre exchange.

"Ah! You two are just in time," cried Darren.

"What for?"

"To give these people their chance — to stop them making fools of themselves — to back me up."

"I don't quite follow," replied Gavin.

"You know — you knew this morning."

"Knew what?"

"Oh! Don't pretend — you don't understand how you got here, either. How either of you got here."

"Gavin, don't answer him!" cried Freya.

Mrs. Rivermore stepped forward. "Mr. Bristow, I see an unpleasant duty will have to be performed. As a rabbi, will you please perform it?"

"What do you want me to do?"

"Take him to the ship's doctor — or the doctor to him."

"I tell you there is no doctor," said Darren forcefully. "But I tell you what you can do if you like — go out there and convince yourself about those lights. Then if I'm wrong — well, I'll go quietly. Rabbi — what do you say?"

Bristow looked hard at him. "If I do it, you'll keep your word?"

"Yes."

"Very well, then." And he strode through the doors to the deck.

Bruce and Peter, who had listened to all this with the fascination of theater-goers at an intriguing play, looked at one another.

"Perhaps we should be getting back to the game," suggested Bruce.

"Wait until I am proved right," insisted Darren.

"What's happened to the rabbi?" Freya demanded.

"He hasn't been gone more than a few seconds," protested Darren.

"Listen," said Peter, caught up in the drama now. "I hear some-one..."

The rabbi entered, gasping as if breathless. He seemed pale and agitated but doing his best to control it.

"Well?" demanded Darren.

"Darren was perfectly right," said Bristow, quietly.

"What?"

"There is no starboard light — no light on the boat at all. And as far as I could see there's nobody anywhere. I'm not even certain that we're moving."

Darren looked at them all. "Ask the steward to come and explain. I spoke to him earlier. It seems we're sailing for both Hell and Heaven."

"Very interesting; that must be a bridge club of course," muttered Gavin.

"We must hurry," exclaimed the rabbi. "While we're talking like this we may be drifting on to the rocks — crashing into something or—?"

"No, sir, we won't do that," the steward remarked from his post behind the bar.

Mrs. Rivermore stalked over to him. "Now look here, my man. Where's the captain? Take me to him!"

"Oh, he left long ago, ma'am."

"Take me to him. You're only a damned waiter, just take me to him."

"Mrs. Rivermore," said the rabbi, putting one hand on her arm. "I think we should all keep our tempers."

The steward nodded. "That's all right, sir; I've known a lot of them to get angry at first."

"A lot of whom?"

"People like you, sir, who are just beginning."

"Beginning?"

"To be passengers."

"What you told me this afternoon was true, wasn't it?" asked Darren.

"That we're dead, sir? Yes, quite true, if that's what you mean."

Mrs. Rivermore turned on her heel. "I need to get in touch with someone at once. Ah, I have it — the radio."

"The ship doesn't carry one, ma'am," replied the steward.

"But I must get out of this — I must get out of it," cried Mrs. Rivermore.

"That, ma'am, is impossible until after the examination."

"What examination?" demanded Darren.

"You'll find out later, sir."

"Gavin!" cried Darren. "Damn it, don't just stand there saying nothing — do something."

"There's no danger, gentlemen and ladies, if that's what you're frightened of," offered the steward.

"How many times have you made this passage, steward?" asked Bristow.

"About five thousand times, sir. I was lost young."

"And it's always been like this?"

"Not always, sir, no. As I was telling this gentleman, the passengers don't find out so quickly, as a rule. I suppose it's because of the half-ways we've got on board this trip."

"Half-ways?"

"Yes, sir, it sometimes does work like that. Of course I can't say anything …"

I looked at my watch and nudged Bruce. "It's really time to get back," I said. "We can watch the next episode of whatever this show is later."

He looked at me strangely for a moment, than nodded briskly. "Right, come on, young Peter," he said.

And we left them to it.

After dinner, we found ourselves drawn once again to the scene of the earlier curious conversations. A small table had been set up near the bar with a water carafe, a glass, and some papers on it. The participants were seated round it in a circle as if for a meeting, and the rabbi seemed to be leading the discussion. Only Gavin and Freya were missing, perhaps still analyzing the boards from the previous session.

"Now, the next thing for us to decide is the most effective way to meet and talk to this examiner. If he is to decide our fates, I suggest I am the one best-fitted to deal with him."

"Don't you think we all ought to speak for ourselves — if we can?" asked Gavin.

"Here's that steward person," proclaimed Mrs. Rivermore. "Why not ask him? He must have met the examiner before."

"You wanted to ask me about the examiner, ma'am?"

"Yes, if you don't mind."

"What did you want to know, exactly?"

"Well, what sort of person is he?"

"I can't say," demurred the steward. "I don't know. It depends on yourselves. I have seen some people before him cry for — no, I can't say."

"Just tell us how we should approach him," the rabbi suggested.

"I have been asked that question nearly five thousand times, sir; I have always answered that it is better to leave the approaching to him."

"Do have I any chance?" asked Darren, plaintively.

"You all have chances, sir," replied the steward.

"Well, at least we can count on the rabbi for some professional advice," Darren mused. "What do you think we should do?"

"I can advise nothing."

"Oh, that's very useful. What, not one word of help?"

"That's different. If I can help, I will. But you mustn't take anything I say to be advice. The blind leading the blind, you know. I can tell you only what I'm going to do myself — and I may be wrong."

"Well, what are you going to do?"

"I have been trying to humbly examine my past; then I am going make one more prayer. But for myself. I cannot pray for others. Perhaps the realization of that is the beginning of my punishment. After all, I've lost my job."

"I don't suppose it paid much, anyway," snarled Darren dismissively. "Appropriate since you don't seem to have been very good at it."

"Oh," cried Freya. "That was the siren. The ship's stopped."

"Exactly. Our judgment moment's arrived."

"No, it can't be. In the bar of a cruise ship?" Darren seemed disbelieving.

"Why shouldn't it be in the bar of a cruise ship? Have any of us really thought much about where and how and when it might be?"

"The examiner is just coming aboard," announced the steward. "He'll be with you in a moment."

A tall, distinguished, and somehow familiar figure loomed in the doorway. "Ah, there you all are. Good morning, everyone."

Bruce looked over at the door with an expression that suggested he was trying hard to recall something. It was as though he vaguely recognized the newcomer but couldn't quite place him in this context.

The rabbi stared. "Well, if it isn't Professor Silver."

Bruce started visibly.

"It is, sir," the professor said, smiling. "Hot here isn't it, though that's to be expected, of course. How are you, Sol? You're looking fit. Have a good passage?"

"I don't feel the heat," replied Bristow.

"I only heard this morning you were due in today — so I hurried down especially to meet you. I've been upcountry."

"Thank you."

"How's my old friend Cardinal? Still playing bridge for a living?"

"No, they've made him a tournament director now."

"Well, I hope he likes it. Do you still go out to Shopsy's after the game? Tell me, what's the pastrami like there now?"

The rabbi coughed. "Look, I'm delighted to see you again, of course, and I'll be happy to chat with you afterwards — if I can — but you must realize, at this moment, how terribly worried we all are?"

"Worried ... about what?"

"This person — whoever it is — who's coming to examine us."

"The examiner! Oh, I shouldn't worry about him! At least I shouldn't worry very much."

"What do you mean?"

"Well, I'm the examiner."

"You — you are?"

"Yes — you're under my orders now," confirmed Silver. "And I tell you, my boy, you'll have to work hard. But I've arranged a room for you in the same place as me. And it's near your work, right in the center of the city, so you couldn't do better, really."

"Work?"

"Yes, I'm afraid you won't be playing bridge anymore. It'll just be work from now on."

"Wait, Professor, you mean I haven't lost my job after all?"

"Of course you haven't lost it. You haven't started it yet."

"Not lost my job? Oh, thank God. I will work harder now, I swear I will, Professor. Where will my congregation be located — Toronto, New York, Miami?"

"Actually, you will have to build your own congregation. We are sending you to Tehran to proselytize the local population and convert them to Judaism."

"Good luck with that, Rabbi," snickered Darren.

"Well, isn't it nice that they know each other so well," Mrs. Rivermore said, and sniffed. "And of course, Mr. Bristow got off lightly. A friend at court, you see. Influence! Hah! It's always the same."

"I'm sure you're feeling better already." The professor smiled at Bristow. "You can start now and help me with this bunch. There aren't many of them."

"That's true. Just Spielman, Mrs. Rivermore, and that nice young couple."

"Then it won't take long and we can get on shore for dinner. Well, let's get to work."

"Can you see the young couple first? I know they must be suffering."

The professor leafed through some papers from his briefcase. "What young couple is this? I've had no information about them. That's strange. Steward, do you know anything about a young couple on this boat?"

"I'm sorry, sir, they'd slipped my mind. They're half-ways, sir."

"Oh, that explains it. All right, let's deal with them right away."

"What's a half-way, Professor?"

"Someone who still has a chance not to go forward, Bristow. You'll see."

"They've gone back to the bridge tournament," announced the steward, after checking around on the deck.

"Perfect," the professor said, and smiled. "Couldn't have asked for a better place to watch them and make a decision. I'll process the other two later."

It was obviously time for me to return, too, for the final rounds. Fascinated by what I had seen and heard, I had missed Bruce and Peter's exit. However, I was spared the trouble of finding them. Professor Silver strode directly over to their table, where Gavin and Freya had just removed their cards from the board.

I resumed my usual seat and watched as Gavin and Freya bid to a pushy slam.

Dealer East; Both vul.

Freya
- ♠ 10 8 4 2
- ♡ 6 4 2
- ◇ A K 6 2
- ♣ A 6

Peter
- ♠ 6
- ♡ 10 5 3
- ◇ 10 7 5 4
- ♣ J 9 5 4 3

```
      N
   W     E
      S
```

Bruce
- ♠ K 7 3
- ♡ K Q J 9 7
- ◇ Q J 8
- ♣ Q 7

Gavin
- ♠ A Q J 9 5
- ♡ A 8
- ◇ 9 3
- ♣ K 10 8 2

Peter	Freya	Bruce	Gavin
		1♡	1♠
pass	2♡	pass	3♣
pass	3◇	pass	3♡
pass	4♣	pass	5♣
pass	6♠	all pass	

"So what decides whether they'll go back?" whispered the rabbi.

"I rather think this time the cards will pass judgment," said the professor gravely.

Peter led the ♡3 and Bruce's jack was allowed to hold. Gavin won the next heart, crossed to dummy with a club and ran the ♠8, which won. He then played the ♠10, covered by the king and won by the ace, and continued with the ♠Q. Next came a diamond to the king to leave this position:

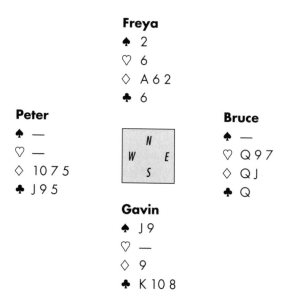

Freya
- ♠ 2
- ♡ 6
- ◇ A 6 2
- ♣ 6

Peter
- ♠ —
- ♡ —
- ◇ 10 7 5
- ♣ J 9 5

Bruce
- ♠ —
- ♡ Q 9 7
- ◇ Q J
- ♣ Q

Gavin
- ♠ J 9
- ♡ —
- ◇ 9
- ♣ K 10 8

At this point Gavin claimed the rest of the tricks. He showed his hand and explained his line of play. "I will ruff the ♡6, and what can Peter do?"

A good question. If West discarded a club, Gavin would play the ♣K, ruff a club, and then return to hand for his club winner via a diamond ruff. If West discarded a diamond, playing the ◇A and ruffing a diamond would establish a good diamond, and then a club ruff would allow declarer to cash his twelfth trick.

I could see the professor was impressed. He tapped Gavin on the shoulder when the round ended. "A word, if I may," he asked.

"And you are…?" asked Gavin.

"Oh, just another ACBL official," the professor replied vaguely, "but I have some good news. Two rooms have opened up in the tournament headquarters hotel — we're making them available to you and your opponents. If you hurry, you'll be able to catch the launch and get settled in."

The foursome hurried off after expressing their thanks. I lingered to hear one final *sotto voce* exchange, as the rabbi asked, "And what would have happened if he hadn't made the slam?"

"I'm very much afraid," replied Professor Silver, "he really would have gone down."

Our little group had grown during the Bronze Life Master's tale, and with its final words, a shiver ran around the circle. The silence lengthened as we thought about what we had heard. Finally, a tall, thin man with close-cropped hair and rimless glasses spoke up.

"Truly a strange tale," he began, "but something almost as bizarre occurred to me a few years ago. By coincidence, it also involved a Nationals in Florida. Let me just get some more coffee, and I'll tell you about it..."

2

DANIEL'S TALE

I had flown down to Tampa by the cheapest route possible, a bus from Toronto to Buffalo and then on to Florida via a brief three-hour lay-over in Charlotte. By the time I got there, it was about nine o'clock in the evening and the moon was coming up in a clear, starry sky over the buildings opposite the airport terminal. The air was unexpectedly chilly and the wind made me shiver — I hadn't expected to need clothes for cold weather, and I wasn't wearing them. The sight of a depressed-looking palm tree assured me that I had indeed arrived at my destination.

"Excuse me," I said to one of the redcaps, "but is there a fairly cheap hotel not too far away from here?'

"Try the Everglades Hotel," the porter answered, pointing down the road. "They might have a room, although hotels are pretty full, what with the football game and the bridge tournament going on. It's about a quarter of a mile along on the other side."

I thanked him, picked up my suitcase, and set off to walk to the Everglades Hotel. I had never been to Tampa before. I didn't know anyone who lived there. But Professor Silver had told me that it was a splendid city, full of wealthy widows who would gladly put me up for a few days as long as I played bridge with them occasionally. I walked briskly down the street, only partly because of the cold. Briskness, Professor Silver had told me, was the one common characteristic of all successful bridge professionals. The big names at the Nationals were absolutely brisk all the time. They were all intimidating in their briskness.

There were no shops on this wide street that I was walking along, only a line of tall houses on each side, all of them identical. They had porches and pillars and four or five steps going up to their front doors, and it was obvious that once upon a time they had been swanky residences. But now, even in the darkness, I could see that the paint was peeling from the woodwork on their doors and windows, and that the handsome white facades were cracked and blotchy from neglect.

Suddenly, in a downstairs window that was brilliantly illuminated by a street lamp not six yards away, I caught sight of a printed notice propped up against the glass in one of the upper panes. It said BED AND BREAKFAST. There was a vase of sunflowers, tall and beautiful, standing just underneath the notice.

I stopped walking. I moved a bit closer. Green curtains (some sort of velvety material) hung on either side of the window. The sunflowers glowed beside them. I went right up and peered through the glass into the room, and the first thing I saw was a bright fire burning in the hearth. There's someone prepared for this weather, I thought. On the carpet in front of the fire, a cute little dachshund was curled up asleep with its nose tucked into its belly. The room itself, so far as I could see in the half-darkness, was filled with comfortable furniture. There was a small piano and a big sofa and several plump armchairs, and in one corner I spotted a large parrot in a cage. Animals were usually a good sign in a place like this, I told myself; all in all, it looked to me as though it would be a pretty decent house to stay in. Certainly, it would be more comfortable than the Everglades Hotel.

On the other hand, a hotel would be more congenial than a boarding house. There would be a bar and perhaps some music in the evenings, and lots of bridge players to talk to, but it would probably be a good bit more expensive, too. I usually stayed in the tournament hotel when I travelled to play bridge. I had never stayed in a boarding house, and, to be perfectly honest, I was a tiny bit frightened of the idea. The name itself conjured up images of watery cabbage, rapacious landladies, and a powerful smell of wet dogs in the living room.

After dithering about like this for two or three minutes, getting colder as I stood there, I finally decided that I would walk on and take a look at the Everglades Hotel before making up my mind. I turned to go.

And now an odd thing happened to me. I was in the act of stepping back and turning away from the window when all at once my eye was caught and held in the most peculiar manner by the small notice that was there. *BED AND BREAKFAST*, it said, *BED AND BREAKFAST, BED AND BREAKFAST, BED AND BREAKFAST*. Each word was like a large black eye staring at me through the glass, holding me, compelling me, forcing me to stay where I was and not to walk away from that house, and the next thing I knew, I was actually moving across from the window to the front door of the house, climbing the steps that led up to it, and reaching for the bell.

I pressed the bell. Far away in the back room I heard it ringing, and then at once (it must have been at once because I hadn't even had time to take my finger from the button) the door swung open and a woman was standing there. Normally, you ring the bell and you have at least a half-minute's wait before the door opens. But this lady was like a jack-in-the-box. I pressed the bell — and out she popped! It made me jump. She was about forty-five or fifty years old, and the moment she saw me, she gave me a warm welcoming smile.

"Please come in," she said pleasantly. She stepped aside, holding the door wide open, and I found myself automatically starting forward into the house. The compulsion or, more accurately, the desire to follow after her into that house was extraordinarily strong.

"I saw the notice in the window," I said, holding myself back.

"Yes, I know."

"I was wondering about a room."

"It's all ready for you, my dear," she said. She had a round pink face and very gentle blue eyes.

"I'm Dan Korbel, here for the bridge," I told her. "I was on my way to the Everglades Hotel, but the notice in your window just happened to catch my eye."

"My dear boy," she said, "why don't you come in out of the cold? The temperature drops so fast once the sun goes down."

"How much do you charge?"

"Twenty five dollars a night, including breakfast."

It was fantastically cheap, less than half of what I had been expecting to pay.

"If that's too much," she added, "then perhaps I can reduce it, just a tiny bit. Do you want to have an egg for breakfast? Eggs are expensive at the moment. It would be two dollars less without the egg."

"Twenty-five dollars is fine," I answered. "I'd like to stay here."

"I knew you would. Come in."

She seemed very nice. She looked like she could be the mother of your best school friend welcoming you into the house for an afternoon of video games. I stepped over the threshold.

"Let me help you with your jacket," she said, hanging it on a nearby peg.

There were no other coats or hats in the hall. There was no luggage — nothing.

"We have it all to ourselves," she said, smiling at me over her shoulder as she led the way upstairs. "You see, it isn't very often I have the pleasure of taking a visitor into my little nest."

She was slightly off, I thought. But at twenty-five bucks a night, who gives a damn about that?

"I would've thought you'd be swamped," I said politely.

"Oh, I am, my dear, I am, of course I am. But the trouble is that I'm inclined to be just a teeny weeny bit choosy and particular — if you see what I mean."

"Ah, yes."

"But I'm always ready. Everything is always ready day and night in this house just on the off-chance that an acceptable young gentleman will come along. And it is such a pleasure, my dear, such a very great pleasure when now and again I open the door and I see someone standing there who is just exactly right." She was halfway up the stairs and she paused with one hand on the stair rail, turning her head and smiling down at me with pale lips. "Like you," she added, and her blue eyes traveled slowly all the way down the length of my body, to my feet, and then up again.

On the first-floor landing she said to me, "This floor is mine." We climbed up a second flight. "And this one is all yours," she said. "Here's your room. I do hope you'll like it." She took me into a small but charming front bedroom, switching on the light as she went in.

"The morning sun comes right in the window, Mr. Perkins. It is Mr. Perkins, isn't it?"

"No," I said. "It's Korbel."

"Mr. Weaver. How nice. I've put fresh sheets on the bed, Mr. Weaver. Your bathroom is down the hall on the right. And you may turn on the heater at any time if you feel chilly."

"Thank you," I said. "Thank you so much." I noticed that the bedspread had been taken off the bed, and that the bedclothes had been neatly turned back on one side, all ready for someone to get in.

"I'm so glad you appeared," she said, looking earnestly into my face. "I was beginning to get worried."

"That's all right," I answered brightly. "There's no need to worry about me." I put my suitcase on the chair and started to open it.

"And what about supper, dear? Did you manage to get anything to eat before you came here?"

"I'm not a bit hungry, thank you," I said. "I think I'll just go to bed as soon as possible because tomorrow I've got to get up early and meet my teammates at the bridge tournament."

"Very well, then. I'll leave you now so that you can unpack. But before you go to bed, would you be kind enough to pop into the sitting room on the ground floor and sign the book? Everyone has to do that because it's the law of the land, and we don't want to go breaking any laws at this stage of the proceedings, do we?" She gave me a little wave of her hand and went quickly out of the room and closed the door.

· · ·

Now, the fact that my landlady appeared to be slightly off her rocker didn't worry me in the least. After all, she was not only clearly harmless — but she was also quite obviously a kind and generous soul. I guessed that she had probably lost a son in the armed forces, or something like that, and had never got over it.

So a few minutes later, after unpacking my suitcase and washing my hands, I sat down on the bed and pulled a piece of paper from my pocket and examined it for the umpteenth time. On it was written the critical hand from the team game I had played a few nights before. It still bothered me, since my client had acerbically remarked that he expected a high-priced expert to make difficult hands. He even said that if he'd wanted someone just to go one down, he could have hired Professor Silver for a lot less money.

Dealer East. EW vul.

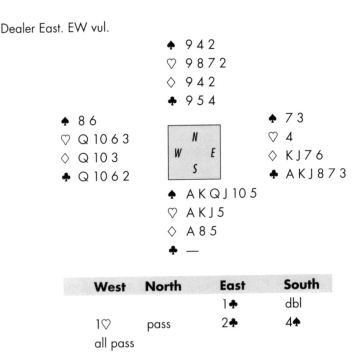

	♠ 9 4 2	
	♡ 9 8 7 2	
	◇ 9 4 2	
	♣ 9 5 4	
♠ 8 6		♠ 7 3
♡ Q 10 6 3		♡ 4
◇ Q 10 3		◇ K J 7 6
♣ Q 10 6 2		♣ A K J 8 7 3
	♠ A K Q J 10 5	
	♡ A K J 5	
	◇ A 8 5	
	♣ —	

West	North	East	South
		1♣	dbl
1♡	pass	2♣	4♠
all pass			

West led a third-highest ♣6 to the king, and I ruffed with the ♠10. After cashing the ♠AK and the ♡A, I played ace and another diamond. The defense cashed another diamond and then played a second club. I ruffed high again, and reached this position:

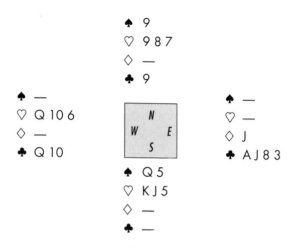

```
              ♠ 9
              ♡ 9 8 7
              ◇ —
              ♣ 9
♠ —                           ♠ —
♡ Q 10 6        N             ♡ —
◇ —           W   E           ◇ J
♣ Q 10          S             ♣ A J 8 3
              ♠ Q 5
              ♡ K J 5
              ◇ —
              ♣ —
```

Perhaps it was the result of three days of tough bridge, but I effectively gave up at that point by playing king and another heart. After all, the auction had told me hearts were 4-1, so I have no idea what I was playing for. But now I saw the winning endgame.

Instead of cashing my heart king, I should have led a low spade to dummy; what could West discard? He is known to have started with ♡Q1063, so a heart pitch makes life easy: I just play king and another heart and my hand is high. But a club is no better: I can ruff dummy's ♣9 in hand then lead the ♡5. West must win and is forced to lead away from his remaining heart honor into my tenace. Making four spades!

Greatly relieved, I decided that I might want a coffee or a little something to eat after all. I trotted downstairs to the ground floor and entered the living room. My landlady wasn't there, but the fire was glowing in the hearth, and the little dachshund was still sleeping in front of it. The room was wonderfully warm and cozy. I lucked out here, I thought, rubbing my hands; this is all right.

I found the guestbook lying open on the piano, so I picked up the pen and wrote down my name and address. There were only two other entries above mine on the page, and, as one always does with guest books, I started to read them. One was a Sami Kehela. The other was an Eric Murray.

That's funny, I thought suddenly. Sami Kehela! It rang a bell. Now where on earth had I heard that rather unusual name before?

Was he a boy at school? No. Was it one of my sister's numerous young men, perhaps, or a friend of my father's? No, no, it wasn't any of those. I glanced down again at the book.

Sami Kehela, Toronto. Eric Murray, Orangeville. Both Canadians too — an odd coincidence.

As a matter of fact, now I came to think of it, I wasn't at all sure that the second name didn't have almost as much of a familiar ring about it as the first.

"Sami Kehela?" I said aloud, searching my memory. "Eric Murray?"

"Such charming men," a voice behind me answered, and I turned and saw my landlady sailing into the room with a large silver tea tray in her hands. She was holding it well out in front of her, and rather high up, as though the tray were a pair of reins on a frisky horse.

"They sound somehow familiar," I said.

"They do? How interesting."

"I'm almost positive I've heard those names before somewhere. Isn't that odd? Maybe it was in the newspapers. They weren't famous in any way, were they? I mean famous hockey players or something like that?"

"Famous," she said, setting the tea tray down on the low table in front of the sofa. "Oh no, I don't think they were famous. But they were extraordinarily handsome, both of them, I can promise you that. They were tall and young and handsome, my dear, just exactly like you."

Once more, I glanced down at the book. "That's odd," I said, noticing the dates. "This last entry is over two years old."

"It is?"

"Yes, indeed. And Sami Kehela is nearly a year before that — more than three years ago."

"Dear me," she said, shaking her head and heaving a dainty little sigh. "I would never have thought it. How time does fly away from us all, doesn't it, Mr. Wilkins?"

"It's Korbel," I said. "K-o-r-b-e-l."

"Oh, of course it is!" she cried, sitting down on the sofa. "How silly of me. I do apologize. In one ear and out the other, that's me, Mr. Korbel."

"You know something?" I said. "Something that's really quite extraordinary about all this?"

"No dear, I don't."

"Well, you see, both those names, Murray and Kehela, I remember them not only separately, so to speak, but somehow or other, in some peculiar way, connected as well. As though they were both famous for the same sort of thing — like … well … Obama and Bush, for example, or Laurel and Hardy."

"How amusing," she said. "But come over here and I'll give you a nice cup of tea and a ginger biscuit before you go to bed."

"That's very kind of you," I said. I stood by the piano watching her as she fussed with the cups and saucers. I noticed that she had small, white, quickly moving hands and red fingernails.

"I'm almost positive it was in the newspapers I saw them," I said. "I'll think of it in a second. I'm sure I will."

There is nothing more tantalizing than a thing like this that lingers just outside the borders of one's memory. I hated to give up.

"Now wait a minute," I said. "Wait just a minute. Kehela … Sami Kehela … wasn't that the name of the Canadian who was a coach at the World Bridge Championships in Argentina the year of the big cheating scandal?"

"Milk?" she said. "And sugar?"

"Yes, please. And then he testified at the inquiry … and Murray … seems to me he played internationally too."

"Bridge championships?" she said. "Oh no, my dear, that can't possibly be right, because my Mr. Kehela was certainly not a bridge player when he came to me. He was a real estate salesman. And Mr. Murray was a bouncer at a local night club. Come over here now and sit next to me. Come on, your tea's all ready for you."

She patted the empty space beside her on the sofa, and she sat there smiling at me and waiting for me to come over.

I crossed the room slowly and sat down on the edge of the sofa. She placed my teacup on the table in front of me.

"There we are," she said. "How nice and cozy this is, isn't it?"

I really don't like tea, but to be polite I raised it to my lips and pretended to drink a little. For half a minute or so, neither of us spoke. But I knew that she was looking at me. Her body was half-turned toward me, and I could feel her eyes resting on my face, watching me over the rim of her teacup. Now and again, I caught a whiff of a peculiar smell that seemed to emanate directly from her person. It was not unpleasant, and it reminded me — well, I wasn't quite sure what it reminded me of. Pickles? New leather? Or was it the corridors of a hospital?

"Mr. Murray was a great one for his tea," she said at length. "Never in my life have I seen anyone drink as much tea as dear, sweet Mr. Murray."

"I suppose he left a while ago," I said. I was still puzzling my head about the two names. I was positive now that I had seen them in the newspapers — in the headlines.

"Left?" she said, arching her brows. "But my dear boy, he never left. He's still here. Mr. Kehela is also here. They're on the third floor, both of them together."

I slowly set down my cup on the table and stared at my landlady. She smiled back at me, and then she put out one of her white hands and patted me comfortingly on the knee.

"How old are you, my dear?" she asked.

"Twenty-four."

"Twenty-four!" she cried. "Oh, it's the perfect age! Mr. Murray was also twenty-four. But I think he was a trifle shorter than you are. In fact, I'm sure he was, and his teeth weren't quite so white. You have the most beautiful teeth, Mr. Weaver, did you know that?"

"They're not as good as they look," I said. "They've got masses of fillings in them at the back."

"Mr. Kehela, of course, was a little older," she said, ignoring my remark. "He was actually twenty-eight. And yet I never would have guessed it if he hadn't told me, never in my whole life. There wasn't a blemish on his body."

"A… what?" I said.

"His skin was just like a baby's."

There was a pause. I picked up my teacup and pretended to take another sip, then I set it down again gently in its saucer. I waited for her to say something else, but she seemed to have lapsed into another of her silences. I sat staring straight ahead into the far corner of the room, biting my lower lip.

"That parrot," I said at last. "You know something? It had me completely fooled when I first saw it through the window from the street. I could have sworn it was alive."

"Alas, no longer."

"It's very clever, the way it's been done," I said. "It doesn't look dead. Who did it?"

"I did."

"You did?"

"Of course," she said. "And you have met my little Basil as well?" She nodded toward the dachshund curled up so comfortably in front of the fire. I looked at it. And suddenly, I realized that this animal had all the time been just as silent and motionless as the parrot. I put out a hand and touched it gently on the top of its back. The back was hard and cold, and when I pushed the hair to one side with his fingers, I could see the skin underneath, greyish-black and dry and perfectly preserved.

"Wow," I said. "That's ... fascinating." I turned away from the dog and stared with deep admiration at the little woman beside me on the sofa. "It must be really difficult to do a thing like that."

"Not in the least," she said. "I stuff all my little pets myself when they pass away. Will you have another cup of tea?"

"No, thank you," I said. The tea smelled faintly of almonds, which was pleasant, but I still didn't much care to drink any of it.

"You did sign the book, didn't you?"

"Oh, yes."

"That's good. Because later on, if I happen to forget what you are called, then I can always come down here and look it up. I still do that almost every day with Mr. Kehela and Mr. ... Mr. ..."

"Murray," I said. "Eric Murray. Excuse my asking, but haven't there been any other guests here except them in the last two or three years?"

Holding her teacup high in one hand, inclining her head slightly to the left, she looked up at me out of the corners of her eyes and gave me another gentle little smile.

"No, my dear," she said. "Only you."

A shudder ran through me, and with that, I rose to my feet and ran out into the street, leaving my stuff behind, not stopping until I reached the welcoming façade of the Everglades Hotel.

It was beginning to feel like one of those campfire nights where everyone tells scary stories. Given our group, it was only a matter of time before someone recounted a tale that was more closely related to bridge, and indeed, we had not long to wait. A thin fellow in a shiny suit and unfortunate tie looked up at us and said, "Hi — my name's Bob, and I'm a bridge professional."

"Hi Bob," we chorused.

Bob went on to express his concerns about playing in the upcoming Nationals. But his fears were not the usual ones — poor cards, lucky opponents, imbecilic clients. No, he spoke of an evil menace who lurked in the side games and directed his minions to thwart the efforts of legitimate experts. This monster was known as "Irving, the Old Man of the Bridge Club," and the bridge professional spoke of him thus.

3

THE BRIDGE PRO'S TALE

The district in which Irving's residence lay was known as Scarborough, signifying in the language of bridge players "the place of the users of Goren's system". In a beautiful valley enclosed between two Tim Hortons drive-throughs, he had constructed a luxurious garden, stored with every delicious fruit and every fragrant shrub that could be procured. Gazebos of various sizes and forms were erected in different parts of the grounds, ornamented by statuary, paintings, and furniture of rich silks. By means of small conduits in these buildings, streams of wine, milk, honey, and even Crown Royal were seen to flow in every direction.

The denizens of these structures were elegant and beautiful damsels, accomplished in the arts of singing, playing all sorts of musical instruments, dancing, and especially dalliance and amorous allurement. Clothed in rich dresses, they were seen continually sporting and amusing themselves in the garden and pavilions. The reason Irving had for building a garden like this was that the bridge god, Sami, had promised to those who followed his teachings the enjoyments of Paradise, where every species of sensual gratification would be found in the society of beautiful nymphs. Irving wanted it understood that he too was a bridge god and the equal of Sami, and also had the power of admitting to Paradise those he chose to favor.

In order that no one might find their way into this delicious valley without his say-so, he constructed a wall around it, through which the only entry was by a secret passage. At his bridge club, Irving entertained a number of youths, selected from the students at the surrounding colleges — young men who showed a disposition for bridge and who appeared to possess the quality of daring courage. With them he was in the daily habit of discoursing on the subject of Paradise and his own power of granting admission. At certain times, he distributed marijuana to ten or a dozen of these youths, and when they were sufficiently stoned, he had them conveyed to the garden.

Upon awakening from this state of lethargy, their senses were struck with all the delightful objects that have been described. Each perceived himself surrounded by lovely damsels, singing, playing, and attracting his regard by the most fascinating caresses, serving him also with sumptuous food and exquisite wines, until, intoxicated with the excess of enjoyment amid actual rivulets of wine and whisky, he believed himself assuredly in Paradise and felt an unwillingness to relinquish its delights. After a few hours, they would be thrown once more into a state of somnolence and carried out of the garden.

Upon being questioned by Irving as to where they had been, their answer was invariably, "In Paradise, thanks to you." Then they would describe the scenes they had witnessed to any bridge players who would listen.

Knowing no better, the young men were thereafter happy to receive Irving's orders and were prepared to do anything for him. The consequence of this system was that when anyone gave offense to Irving, they were publicly humiliated by these assassins, none of whom felt at risk of retaliation, since they held little regard for their own reputation and even their masterpoint holdings, provided they could please Irving. So his tyranny became the subject of dread in all the bridge tournaments of North America.

Eventually, I myself provoked the ire of the monster.

I was playing with a client at the last Toronto Regional when Irving arrived at my table. We picked up an interesting hand.

Dealer South. Both vul.

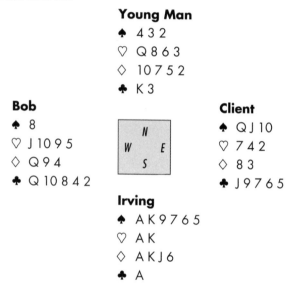

Young Man
♠ 4 3 2
♡ Q 8 6 3
◇ 10 7 5 2
♣ K 3

Bob
♠ 8
♡ J 10 9 5
◇ Q 9 4
♣ Q 10 8 4 2

Client
♠ Q J 10
♡ 7 4 2
◇ 8 3
♣ J 9 7 6 5

Irving
♠ A K 9 7 6 5
♡ A K
◇ A K J 6
♣ A

Bob	Young Man	Client	Irving
			2♣
pass	2◇	pass	2♠
pass	3NT[1]	pass	4NT*
pass	5♣*	pass	5◇*
pass	5♠*	pass	6♠
all pass			

1. Three-card raise, 5-7 HCP.

I led the ♡J, won by South's ace. Irving cashed the ♠AK, revealing that East had a trump trick. Now he played the ◇A and ◇K, and when the queen did not drop, he conceded one down.

"Too bad. Once spades were 3-1, I needed the diamond queen to be singleton or doubleton. Not a bad slam — well over fifty percent — just an unlucky hand," said Irving.

"Actually not," I said recklessly. "It's closer to a seventy-five percent slam and it actually makes as the cards lie."

"How so? Please explain, Mr. Expert," said Irving, beginning to glower.

"After you've got the bad news in trumps, cash the ace and king of diamonds, the heart ace and king and the club ace, and then exit with a trump. This still wins if there is a singleton or doubleton diamond queen. But if East has a singleton or doubleton diamond, he is end-played. The total chance is better than seventy percent. In this instance, East has only two diamonds and when he wins the trump queen he has to lead a club or a heart, providing you with a stepping stone to the dummy for two discards!"

One of the kibitzers giggled and Irving thanked me malevolently as he stalked off.

A few weeks later, I was playing in the finals of the Ontario Team Trials. I estimated that we had a comfortable lead over the strange-looking team we had drawn. They were a quartet of bearded young men who played well but were wildly aggressive in their bidding. Our opponents for this set had introduced themselves as Omar and Nidal. As the session played out, they got lucky on some deals, and gradually reduced the deficit. The last hand dissolved our lead and was the cause of acrimonious criticism afterwards from our teammates.

Nidal brushed aside the preempt and simply bid a club slam.

Omar
♠ A 8 4 3
♡ A Q 6
◇ J 5 3 2
♣ J 3

Client
♠ K Q J 9 7 2
♡ J 4 3 2
◇ K
♣ K 10

N
W   E
S

Bob
♠ 6 5
♡ 10 7 5
◇ 10 8 7 6
♣ Q 8 6 2

Nidal
♠ 10
♡ K 9 8
◇ A Q 9 4
♣ A 9 7 5 4

Client	Omar	Bob	Nidal
2♠	pass	pass	6♣
all pass			

After winning the ♠K lead, he played a diamond to the ace (dropping West's singleton king) while remarking, "Eight never, nine ever," and then led a small club from his hand. West won the ♣K and continued with the ♠Q. Nidal ruffed, played a heart to dummy, and ran the ♣J. When the ♣10 appeared, he cashed the red suits, ending in dummy, and then led a spade and couped my ♣Q8.

Our partners came back with minus 300 having bid 3NT and taken the diamond finesse at Trick 2, giving us a net loss of 18 IMPs, wiping out our lead, and knocking us out of the event. While we were discussing how to assign blame for this disastrous hand, Nidal appeared with the scoreslip for me to initial.

"There was nothing you could have done," he said. "It was written."

"Written?" I echoed.

He smiled and said, "It was the will of Irving."

And then he disappeared into the crowd.

"Enough fairy stories," announced a no-nonsense woman who was sitting on a sofa across from the coffee machine. *"I'm going to tell you a real one. It begins with a conversation after an afternoon duplicate at our club…"*

4

THE WIFE OF BATHURST STREET'S TALE

For some reason, any time the afternoon bridge players assembled, they turned into giggling schoolgirls. As soon as they gathered together, they went into their routine. After flexing their imaginations with stories of what the bridge pros had been getting up to with their clients, they started on each other. Then it was never long before the topic of Natalie's "secret lover" came up. I'd just asked her if she would be bringing him to the Nationals. She managed a coy smile and said, "What are you talking about,?" Everyone giggled.

Macdonald Bird was an inoffensive, harassed-looking man in his late thirties who happened to walk into the bridge club one afternoon looking for a partner for the duplicate game. None of the regular players had arrived without a partner, so Natalie had played with him herself. They had a pleasant game, although her partner was not as good a bridge player as he obviously fancied himself to be. Natalie, on the other hand, played well above her usual level.

Macdonald Bird
♠ A 9 2
♡ A 10 9
◇ K J 6 5
♣ 9 3 2

LHO
♠ 8 6 5 4 3
♡ J
◇ 4 3 2
♣ K J 7 4

	N	
W		E
	S	

RHO
♠ —
♡ K 9 7 6 4 2
◇ 10 9 8 7
♣ 10 8 6

Natalie
♠ K Q J 10 7
♡ Q 5 3
◇ A Q
♣ A Q 5

LHO	Bird	RHO	Natalie
	1◇	2♡	2♠
pass	3♠	pass	4♣
pass	4♡	pass	4NT*
pass	5♡*	pass	6♠
all pass			

The ♡J was led and Natalie made the surefire play of winning the ♡A and dropping the ♡Q from her hand. Then she drew trumps, throwing two low clubs from the table. The ◇AQ and a heart to the nine followed. Whether East won or ducked, there was a heart entry to the two good diamonds in dummy. Her partner congratulated her on her expert dummy play and sent admiring glances over the table for the rest of the afternoon. After the game, Natalie and Macdonald lingered over a coffee, during which time he asked numerous questions of her, which she answered with tact and candor.

Natalie thought no more about him until two weeks later, when she reported for duty to the neighborhood medical clinic at which she volunteered three mornings a week. She was told that a man had been asking for her and would be calling back next morning. Understandably, this created some lively interest in the clinic, particularly when he arrived at five minutes to noon carrying a bunch of roses.

At thirty-three, Natalie's the second youngest of the female players at the club. She exercises and diets and colors her hair with blond highlights, and she's popular with many of the men who go to the clinic and bridge club, but she was not used to floral tributes. Under the amused and frankly envious observation of the nurses in the clinic, Natalie had blushingly accepted the flowers, trying to explain that such a tribute was unnecessary, charming as it was.

However, later that evening Macdonald followed up the flowers by approaching her at the bridge club and insisting that she give up any idea of playing that evening and instead join him for dinner at the China House restaurant. She found him difficult to refuse. One of the other girls gave her an unseen nudge and planted her purse in her hand.

"So that was the start of the long-running joke about your secret lover?" I asked Natalie.

"Really, the joke is on the others," she replied. "They haven't guessed it in their wildest fantasies, but things have developed to the extent that now I really am sleeping with him regularly.

"Oh, don't look so shocked, Professor, and don't assume too much about the relationship, either. Sit here beside me so the whole club can't hear," she continued. "In the common understanding of the word, he's not my lover. Sleeping together and making love are not necessarily the same thing."

As I listened, I realized that her situation wasn't entirely as the girls in the bridge club might have imagined it. Natalie had learned over that first cocktail in the China House that Macdonald had a job as a freelance writer that entailed his traveling a great deal, typically in southern Ontario and parts of the United States. He visited Toronto for an overnight stay every two weeks. He liked traveling, yet he admitted that the nights away from home had been instrumental in the failure of his marriage. However, as he altruistically put it, he couldn't really blame a wife who sought companionship elsewhere when her husband spent every other week away on business.

The first outing with Natalie led to another when Macdonald was next in the city. Two weeks later, Natalie had invited him to her apartment for a "spot of supper," explaining that it was no trouble, because you could do much more interesting things cooking for two than alone. Macdonald had heaped praise on her chicken *cordon bleu*, and after that the evening meal had become a fortnightly fixture. On the first occasion, he had properly returned to his hotel at the end of the evening, but the following time, he had shown Natalie a hand he had played recently and they both got so engrossed that neither of them had noticed the time until it was well after midnight.

"It must have been an interesting hand," I said.

"Oh yes, perhaps you would like to see it? Macdonald failed to make the contract and was very upset when one of the opponents said that it was makeable and then left the table without explaining further. Here it is."

Dealer North. EW vul.

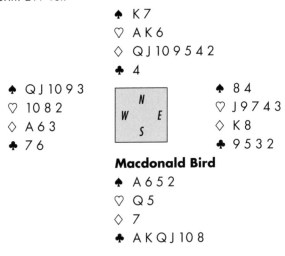

```
                    ♠ K 7
                    ♡ A K 6
                    ◇ Q J 10 9 5 4 2
                    ♣ 4
  ♠ Q J 10 9 3                          ♠ 8 4
  ♡ 10 8 2            N                  ♡ J 9 7 4 3
  ◇ A 6 3        W        E              ◇ K 8
  ♣ 7 6               S                  ♣ 9 5 3 2
```

Macdonald Bird
```
                    ♠ A 6 5 2
                    ♡ Q 5
                    ◇ 7
                    ♣ A K Q J 10 8
```

West	North	East	Bird
	1◇	pass	2♣
pass	2◇	pass	2♠
pass	3◇	pass	3♡
pass	3NT	pass	4♣
pass	4♡	pass	6♣
all pass			

"Macdonald won the spade lead in the dummy and immediately played ace and another spade, attempting to ruff the third spade in the dummy. This got overruffed and a diamond was returned, West cashing the ace of diamonds and the spade jack for two down."

"Ruff in haste, repent at leisure," I said, after examining the hand for a few moments. "Bird should have hoped the clubs were no worse than 4-2 and that diamonds were 3-2 (or that East has $\diamond$AKxx or West a singleton $\diamond$A or $\diamond$K), about sixty-nine percent — much better than trying to ruff a spade, which is less than sixty-two percent.

"So, as he needed to preserve entries to dummy, he should have called for the ♠7 and won with the ♠A. Then he could have played four top clubs, discarding two diamonds and the ♡6! Next, he could have led a diamond to the nine and king. East would have returned a spade to dummy's king and declarer would have ruffed a diamond. Then a heart to the king would be followed by a second diamond ruff, dropping the ace to set up the suit. Dummy is high when a heart is played to the king. I think quite a few players would be seduced by the ♡Q!"

"Thanks! We never did figure out what the guy meant," Natalie said. "Anyway," she continued, resuming her story, "I felt so relaxed and safe with him that it seemed the most natural thing in the world to make up the spare bed for him and invite him to stay the night. There'd been no suggestion from either of us of a more intimate arrangement. That's what I liked about Macdonald. He wasn't one of those predatory males. He was enough of a gentleman to suppress his natural physical instincts. And one night six weeks later, during a thunderstorm, I tapped on his bedroom door and said I was feeling frightened. He offered, in the same gentlemanly spirit, to come to my room until the storm abated. As it happened, I still slept in the same king-size double bed I got used to when I was married, so there was room for Macdonald without us touching. We fell asleep listening for the thunder. By then, it was the season of summer storms, so the next time he came to the apartment, we agreed that it was a sensible precaution to sleep together even when the sky was clear. You can never be sure when a storm might blow up during the night. And when the first chill nights of autumn arrived, neither of us liked the prospect of sleeping apart between cool sheets. Besides, as Macdonald considerately mentioned, using one bed made for less laundry.

"Speaking of laundry, I had taken to washing out his shirts, underwear, and pajamas. I even bought him a special pair of bottle-green French pajamas with an elastic waistband and no buttons. They were waiting on his pillow, washed and ironed, each time he visited. He was very appreciative. He always arrived with a bottle of French wine that we drank with our meal. Once or twice he told me that he would have taken me out to a restaurant, but my cooking was so excellent that it would have shown up the chef. He particularly relished the cooked breakfast that I produced before he went on his way in the morning.

"A couple of weeks ago, I arrived home from an afternoon bridge game to find a greeting card in my mailbox. I'd forgotten my birthday was on Sunday. Living alone, with no family, I tend to ignore such occasions. But someone had obviously decided this one should not go by unnoticed. I didn't recognize the handwriting, and the postmark was too faint to read. I opened and smiled. A print of a single rose, and inside, under the printed birthday greeting, the handwritten letter **M**.

"I didn't recognize Macdonald's handwriting because that was the first time I had seen it. He wasn't one for sending letters. And the return address wouldn't have given me a clue because I didn't know where he lived. He was vague or dismissive when it came to personal information, so I never pressed him. He was entitled to his privacy. I couldn't help wondering sometimes, and my best guess was that since the failure of his marriage, he had tended to neglect himself and his home and devote himself to his job and to bridge. He lived for the traveling and for his bridge games, and, I led myself to believe, his biweekly visits to North Toronto.

"A little later that day, the doorbell rang. I opened the door to find a woman, dark-haired, about my age, pretty, with one of those long, elegant faces with high cheekbones that you see in French films. She wore a dark blue suit and a white blouse buttoned to the neck as if she were attending an interview for a job. Mainly, I was aware of her gray-green eyes scrutinizing me with an interest unusual in people who called casually at the door."

"So who was she?" I asked Natalie.

She told me that the woman had confirmed with her that she was indeed Mrs. Natalie Dormer and then introduced herself as Tracey Gibbons. Natalie hadn't heard of her. Ms. Gibbons had shaken her head and was apparently not surprised.

"I don't know what you're going to think of me," Ms. Gibbons said, "coming to your apartment like this, but it's reached the point where something has to be done. It's about your husband."

Natalie was confused. "My husband?" she asked. She hadn't heard from Stanley in seven years.

"May I come in?"

"I guess you'd better."

Natalie showed her into the living room and couldn't help but wonder if this was some sort of scam. The woman's eyes blatantly surveyed the room, the furniture, the ornaments, everything.

"I think you'd better come to the point, Ms. Gibbons."

"It's Mrs., actually, not that it matters. I'm waiting for my divorce to come through." Suddenly, the woman sounded nervous and defensive. "I'm not promiscuous. I want you to understand that, Mrs. Dormer, whatever you think of me. And I'm not deceitful, either, or I wouldn't be here. I want to get things straight between us. I've driven over from Hamilton today to talk to you."

Natalie was beginning to understand what this was all about. Mrs. Gibbons was having a relationship with Stanley, and for some obscure reason she felt obliged to confess it to his ex-wife. Clearly, the poor woman was in a state of nerves, so it was kindest to let her say her piece before gently showing her to the door.

"You probably wonder how I got your address," Mrs. Gibbons went on. "He doesn't know I'm here. I promise you. It's only over the last few weeks that I began to suspect he had a wife. Certain things you notice, like his freshly ironed shirts. He left his suitcase open the last time he came, and I happened to see the birthday card he addressed to you. That's how I got your address."

"Which card?"

"The rose. I looked inside, I'm ashamed to admit. I had to know." Mrs. Gibbons sighed.

With a start, Natalie realized the woman wasn't talking about Stanley at all, but Macdonald, *her* Macdonald.

"My head was spinning," she told me. "I thought I was going to faint. I said, 'I think I need a drink.'"

Mrs. Gibbons nodded. "I'll join you if I may."

When Natalie handed over the glass, she said to the woman, "You are talking about a man named Macdonald?"

"Of course!"

"He's not my husband."

"What?" Mrs. Gibbons appeared disbelieving.

"He visits me sometimes."

"And you wash his shirts?"

"Usually."

"The bastard!" said Mrs. Gibbons, her eyes brimming. "The rotten, two-timing bastard! I knew there was someone else, but I thought it was his wife he was so secretive about. I persuaded myself that he was unhappily married and I came here to plead with you to let him go. I could kill him."

"How do you think I feel? I didn't even know there was anyone else in his life."

"Does he keep a toothbrush and a razor in your bathroom?"

"And a hand towel as well."

"And I suppose you bought him some expensive aftershave lotion?" Mrs. Gibbons asked Natalie.

Natalie confirmed it bitterly. In her outraged state, she needed to talk, and sharing the trouble seemed likely to dull the pain. She related how she and Macdonald had met and how she had invited him home. Mrs. Gibbons said, 'And one thing led to another? When I think of what I was induced to do in the belief that I was the love of his life …'"

"It was expensive, too," Natalie told her.

"Expensive?" Mrs. Gibbons queried.

"Making three-course dinners and large cooked breakfasts."

"I wasn't talking about cooking," said Mrs. Gibbons.

"Ah," Natalie said, in an attempt to convey that she understood exactly what Mrs. Gibbons was talking about.

"Things I didn't get up to in ten years of marriage to a very athletic man," Mrs. Gibbons further confided. "But you know all about it. Casanova was a boy scout compared to Macdonald. God, I feel so humiliated."

"Would you like another drink, Mrs. Gibbons?" Natalie asked her guest.

"Why don't you call me Tracey?" suggested Mrs. Gibbons, holding out her glass. "We're just his playthings, you and I. How many others are there, do you suppose?"

"Who knows?" Natalie said. "There are plenty of divorced women like you and me, pathetically grateful for any attention that comes our way. Let's face it: we're secondhand goods."

"What are we going to do with him?"

"Kick him out with his toothbrush and hand towel, I suppose," Natalie answered inadequately.

"So he finds other deluded women to prey on?" said Tracey. "That's not the treatment for the kind of animal we're dealing with. Personally, I feel so angry and abused that I would kill him if I knew how to get away with it. Wouldn't you?"

Natalie told me she was stunned. "Are you serious?" she asked.

"Totally," said Mrs. Gibbons. "He's ruined my hopes and every atom of self-respect I had left. What was I to him? His bit in Hamilton, his Monday night amusement."

"And I was Tuesday night in Toronto." Natalie was suddenly given a cruel and vivid understanding of the way she had been used. Sex was Monday, supper Tuesday. In her own way she felt just as violated as Tracey. An arrangement that had seemed to be considerate and beautiful was revealed as cynically expedient. The reason he had never touched her was that he was always satiated after his night of unbridled passion in Hamilton.

"Tracey," said Natalie, deciding, "if you know of a way to kill him, I know how to get away with it."

The women talked for hours. For the plan to work, they had to devise a way of killing without mess. The body should not be marked by violence. They debated various ways of dispatching a man. Whether the intention was serious or not, Natalie found that just talking about it was a balm for the pain that Macdonald had inflicted on her. She and Tracey agreed to take no action until they had time to adjust to the shock, but they were adamant that they would meet again.

"And did you meet again?" I asked.

"Oh yes! She called me the following Monday evening," Natalie said excitedly. "She'd been doing some research and she didn't want to be specific over the phone, but she knew where to get some stuff that would do the job. It was simple, quick, and very effective, and the best thing about it was that she could get it at work.

Natalie recalled that Tracey had said that she worked for a company that manufactured agricultural fertilizers. She guessed she was talking about some chemical substance. Poison.

"The thing is," Tracey went on, "if I get some, are you willing to do your part? You said it would be no problem."

"That's true, but…"

"By the weekend? He's due to visit me on Monday."

Natalie sighed. The reminder of Macdonald's Monday assignations in Hamilton was like a stab of pain to her. She told Tracy to come over about the same time as the previous Saturday and promised to do her part.

The part she was to play in the killing of Macdonald was to obtain a blank death certificate from one of the doctors at the clinic where she volunteered. She'd often noticed how careless Dr. Thorndyke was with his paperwork. He was the oldest of the five practitioners and his desk was always in disorder. Natalie waited most of the week for an opportunity. On Friday morning she had to go into his office to ask him to clarify his handwriting on a prescription form. The death certificate pad was there on the credenza. At quarter after eleven, when the doctor went out on his rounds and Natalie was on duty with one other girl, she slipped back into his office. No one saw her.

"And did Tracey show up on Saturday?" I asked.

"Yes, she came to my door and told me she had traveled by train to Toronto. She didn't want to leave her car outside my building again," she explained.

"Smart move," I replied. "It's surprising how much people notice."

"Sensible," Natalie agreed. "I told her I wanted to hear about the stuff she had got and if it was really going to work."

Tracey had smiled. "Darling, it's foolproof. Do you want to see it?" She had opened her handbag and taken out a small brown glass bottle. "Pure nicotine. We use it at work."

"Nicotine?" Natalie said. "Is it a poison?"

"Deadly."

"There isn't much here."

"The fatal dose is measured in milligrams," Tracey informed her. "A few drops will do the trick."

"How can we get him to take it?"

"I've thought of that." Tracey smiled. "You're going to like this. In a glass of his favorite beer. Nicotine goes yellow on exposure to light and air, and there's a bitter taste, which the ale will mask."

"How does it work?"

"It acts like a massive stimulant. The vital organs simply can't withstand it. He'll die of cardiac arrest in a very short time. Did you bring the death certificate?"

Natalie placed the bottle on the kitchen table and opened one of the cookbooks. The certificate was inside.

"You're careful too," Tracey said approvingly. "I brought a prescription from the doctor to copy the signature from, as you suggested. What else do we have to fill in here? **Name of deceased**. What shall we call him?

"Anything but Macdonald," Natalie said. "How about Harvey? Harvey … Jones."

"All right. Harvey Jones it is. **Date of death.** I'd better fill that in after the event. What shall we put as cause of death? Cardiac failure?"

"No, that's likely to be a sudden death," Natalie said, replied thinking of post-mortems. "Bronchial pneumonia is better."

"Suits me," said Tracey writing it down. "After he's dead, I take this to the funeral parlor in Hamilton, and tell them that Harvey Jones was my brother, is that right?"

"Yes, it's very straightforward. They'll want his date of birth and one or two other details that you can invent. Then they take over after that."

"I ask for a cremation, of course. Will it cost much?" Tracey asked.

"Don't worry. He can afford it."

"Too true," said Tracey, "his wallet is always stuffed with bills."

"He never has to spend much," Natalie pointed out. "The way he runs his life, he gets everything he wants for nothing."

"The bastard."

"You really mean to do it, don't you?"

Tracey stood up and looked steadily at Natalie. "On Monday evening, when he comes to me. I'll phone you when it's done."

"The first thing I'm going to do is burn those pajamas," Natalie said.

Tracey remarked, "He never wore pajamas with me."

"Really?" Natalie's curiosity was aroused. "What exactly did he do with you? Are you able to talk about it?

"I don't believe I could," Tracey said quietly.

"If I poured you another drink? We are in this together now."

"Oh, all right," said Tracey with a sigh.

. . .

And that was as far as we got in the story before both Natalie and I had to part ways that day.

Sunday seemed the longest day of Natalie's life, she said, but she finally got through it. On Monday she didn't go to work but was so nervous she phoned me and asked me to play duplicate with her while she waited for the phone call.

"Natalie, you've made me an accessory to your crime. Aren't you afraid I might go to the police?" I asked her as we walked toward our table.

"Oh no," she said, and smiled. "If you ever breathe a word I'll tell your husband about what you get up to without him at tournaments. And when he gets through with you, you'll be living on the street for the rest of your life."

The call came almost immediately afterwards, and Natalie snatched up her cellphone.

"I'll put it on speaker phone so you can hear."

"Hello, Natalie," said the voice on the phone.

"*It's Macdonald!*" Natalie mouthed to me.

She spoke into the telephone, "Macdonald?"

"Yes. Not like me to call you on a Monday, is it? The fact is, I happen to be in Hamilton on my travels, and it occurred to me that I can be in Toronto in half an hour if you're free this evening."

"Has something happened?" Natalie asked him.

"No, my dear. Just a change of plans. I won't expect much of a meal."

"That's good, because I haven't got one for you," Natalie told him.

There was a moment's hesitation before he said. "Are you all right? You don't sound quite yourself."

"Don't I?" Natalie said flatly. "Well, I've had a bit of a shock. My sister died here Saturday. It was quite unexpected. Bronchial pneumonia. I've had to do everything myself. She's being cremated on Wednesday."

"Your sister? Natalie, I'm terribly sorry. I didn't even know you had a sister."

"Her name was Olive. Olive Jones," said Natalie, and she couldn't help smiling at her own resourcefulness. After she had poisoned Tracey with a drop of nicotine in her brandy, all it had needed on the death certificate was a couple of touches of the pen.

"We weren't close. I'm not too distressed. Yes, why don't you come over, it will help me relax," she continued.

"You're sure you want me?" inquired Macdonald.

"Oh, I want you," answered Natalie. "Yes, I definitely want you."

She terminated the call and turned to me and said, "Looks like our bridge game is off, I'm sorry."

"Quite understandable," I replied. "I guess you have some grocery shopping to do?"

"Oh, no!" Natalie said to me. "I'm going to Victoria's Secret to pick out a black negligée."

"A pretty fantasy," commented a fair-haired middle-aged gentleman who had so far contributed little to our conversation. He had selected a seat strategically placed by the coffee, but now leaned forward to be better heard. "Fortunately for you all, I'm not the litigious type. Let me introduce myself — the name is Bird, Macdonald Bird."

We all looked at him with heightened interest, especially the women.

"And before you ask, I'm often confused with my third cousin in England, a scribbler whose name is attached to hundreds of books on bridge, mostly indistinguishable one from another. I'm also a writer, as you have just heard — perhaps the only detail in the story that is not fictional. But I don't write about bridge; I'm a freelance crime writer. Let me tell you another story of murder, but in this case, a story that has the attraction of being true. I know this because I was myself involved in discovering the guilty party…"

5

MACDONALD BIRD'S TALE

The first few days of the Toronto Nationals were progressing much as usual. That, at any rate, was the impression I got when I found myself unaccountably elbowing my way to free hot dogs after the evening session on the fourth Saturday in July 2011.

I don't like parties much, even those with alcohol; nor do I like bridge players much. For that matter, bridge players generally like me even less. Either they don't know how I play, or if they do know, they have little respect for my game and often let me know it. So I took myself and my beer bottle into a corner and surveyed the attendees with distaste.

Like gravitates to like. A woman, obviously as lonely as me but wearing, in place of a surly frown, a fixed and determined smile, edged her way into my corner. She was somewhat faded, middle-aged — someone who probably had once been prettier. Her clothes were worn as wrongly as female bridge players can wear clothes, but unlike most of theirs, hers were expensive. She was clearly out of place, and I decided that behind the fixed smile she was unhappy.

"Do you want to get out of here?" I said suddenly. "I do. Let's go."

The woman started. "Go somewhere else?" she repeated vaguely. "Oh, no! I think it's wonderful!"

"Do you?" I replied glumly. "What in particular?"

"Oh, well … everything. I mean, all these enthusiasts and … and experts and professionals. Oh, I wish I could play well. Are you an expert?"

"No," I said firmly.

"It must be wonderful to be able to play really well. Mr. Banditti says he believes I could if I just worked harder at it. Er … you know Frank Banditti, of course?"

She asked this in such an appealing manner that, to my surprise, I succumbed. "Of course."

She's in love with him, I thought without enthusiasm, noting the pleasure, singularly tinged with relief, that at once illuminated her face. I wondered who this Banditti was and why he wasn't looking after his client, and prepared for the worst.

And I received it. A flood of Mr. Banditti promptly poured over me.

"Mr. Banditti says..." Indeed, I wondered how Mr. Banditti was able to get many words in at all.

But anything that falls into a crime journalist's trashcan has potential. I began planning a short story. It would be called "Mr. Banditti Says..." and it would be about … well, it would be partly about Mr. Banditti.

"By the way, how was your game today?" she asked.

"Not bad, though I'm upset about one hand I played. I have a feeling I should have made my contract, but I can't think how. I was just going over the hand but I can't find the winning line of play, even double-dummy."

```
              ♠ A K 8
              ♡ 5
              ◇ K 9 6 4 2
              ♣ A Q 8 5

♠ Q 6 3 2          N          ♠ 4
♡ K Q J 9                     ♡ 10 7 6 4 2
◇ J 5 3        W       E      ◇ Q 8
♣ 9 4              S          ♣ J 10 7 3 2

              Me
              ♠ J 10 9 7 5
              ♡ A 8 3
              ◇ A 10 7
              ♣ K 6
```

West	North	East	South
			1♠
pass	2◇	pass	2NT
pass	3♠	pass	4♠
pass	4NT*	pass	5♡*
pass	6♠	all pass	

"I won the ace of hearts and ruffed a heart low in the dummy. I cashed the two top spades, noting that East showed out, playing a small club. Then I played dummy's ace and queen of clubs, throwing my last heart on the queen. I'd expected a club-diamond squeeze on East, but West ruffed the queen of clubs with a low spade and then cashed his trump queen. The opponents subsequently came to a diamond trick for two down. With the 4-1 trump split, and the squeeze not working, I just can't see a winning line of play."

"I watched Frank play this hand and he made it easily," she said.

Naturally, I thought. "How did he play it?"

"He won the ace of hearts and ruffed a heart high. Then he played a club to the king and ruffed another heart high. After that, he led dummy's eight of spades to the nine in his hand. West won, but couldn't beat the contract."

"I see," I said. "Is Mr. Banditti here?"

"Oh, yes," the woman said eagerly, "he's over there." Her glance appeared to indicate a group of three bearded men, one tall, one short, and one middling. I had no idea of Mr. Banditti's height. I couldn't decide whether he should be the tall, cadaverous young man, the short, bouncing young man, or the middling, might-be-anything young man.

There must be a triangle, of course. Her husband...

"My husband isn't much interested in bridge," the woman supplied, rather wistfully.

"Of course not," I said with gratitude. No, of course the husband mustn't be interested. The husband must be a self-made man: a self-opinionated, self-satisfied man, who...

"You see, my husband doesn't like me to go to tournaments without him, and he doesn't want to go himself."

"Exactly!" So he rules his wife out of school as well as in and won't let her go to tournaments. Excellent. Probably a short, pompous little man.

"How tall is your husband?" I asked abruptly.

The woman looked taken aback. "How tall? Well, I don't know."

"Surely you know whether your husband's tall or short," I said impatiently. Ridiculous woman! It was important that the husband be short, because then Mr. Banditti could be the tall, cadaverous man.

"I think he's just about ... average."

"In a country of dwarves, the average man is a giant," I said, inaccurately as well as inanely; but I judged that this was the sort of thing that the woman attended tournament parties to hear, and it would've been a pity if she didn't have didn't have at least one gem to carry away with her.

The woman uttered a sudden exclamation and made a rush for the door. Through the doorway, I caught a glimpse of a blond head throwing an abrupt nod in her direction, and Mr. Banditti passed, the secret of his identity still unsolved. All three men had been fair-haired.

"Gentlemen prefer to be blonds," I muttered sourly.

"Was that an epigram, my sweet?" asked a familiar voice.

"Natalie!" I exclaimed with relief. "Fancy seeing you in this bear pit. And speaking of bears, do you know a Mr. Banditti?"

"Frank Banditti? Yes. He's sort of a Flight B pro — doesn't make much money at it, so he tries to hang around with people who have money."

"He's a sponger?" I asked delightedly. Oh, admirable: sponging, cadaverous Mr. Banditti, taking the wives of pompous, average self-made men to tournaments (wife paying)!

"I would say so. Why are you so pleased about it?"

"Because it fits so nicely. Tell me more of this Banditti."

"I don't know that there's much more to tell," Natalie said. "He specializes in playing with the wives of rich men. A bridge gigolo, you might call him. I hear he's got hold of some groceress now and is playing with her everywhere."

"*Groceress*, Natalie?"

"The feminine of 'grocer'! I understand that the husband is a big noise in supermarkets."

"It's perfect!" I said ecstatically. "I'll write the story this evening."

But more pressing tasks intervened and I did not write the story that evening, or any evening, and within a week I'd forgotten the very name of Banditti. But Mr. Banditti's story was being written nonetheless, in a different city by a different hand and in a different medium.

I've said that I'm a freelance writer specializing in crime stories; I get material by cultivating contacts in various police forces. I was in New England a couple of years later for the Summer Nationals, combining business with pleasure by playing in a side game with the local chief of police. The chief, whatever his talents in law enforcement might be, was a terrible bridge player. There was a rumor that from time to time he would order the arrest of a bridge expert on trumped-up charges and then release them in exchange for the promise of a game the next evening. Apparently, this source of partners was drying up, as more and more of them preferred to remain in jail rather than sit opposite him at a bridge table. I soon discovered why.

Dealer South. Both vul.

Bird
- ♠ 8 5 2
- ♡ 10 9 8 4
- ◊ A 7 6 4
- ♣ 8 4

West
- ♠ J 10 9 7
- ♡ Q 7 6 2
- ◊ Q 10 5
- ♣ 7 5

```
      N
   W     E
      S
```

East
- ♠ K Q 6 4 3
- ♡ —
- ◊ J 9 8
- ♣ 10 9 6 3 2

Chief
- ♠ A
- ♡ A K J 5 3
- ◊ K 3 2
- ♣ A K Q J

West	North	East	South
			2♣
pass	2◊	pass	2♡
pass	3♡	pass	3♠
pass	4◊	pass	4NT*
pass	5◊*	pass	5♠*
pass	6♡	all pass	

The chief won the opening spade lead with his ace and immediately laid down the ♡A, getting the bad news as East showed out. He attempted to recover by discarding diamonds from the dummy on his clubs. But West ruffed the third club low, and now the chief had to lose the ♡Q and an inevitable diamond, going one down.

"I needed West to hold four clubs so I could pitch a couple of diamonds from dummy and engineer a third round diamond ruff," lamented the chief.

"Well, the contract was makeable, just not that way," I said tactfully.

"How? Seems impossible on the lie of the cards."

"If you plan to touch trumps at Trick 2, then the card to lead is the jack of hearts. If West takes it with the queen, you organize two spade ruffs in your hand with the ace and king of hearts. This is called a dummy reversal — you subsequently draw trumps with dummy's hearts and you discard your diamond loser on the last trump. If he ducks the jack, cash the ace and king of trumps and run your clubs, throwing two diamond losers away. West is welcome to ruff a club with his only remaining trump, the queen, as you discard a diamond. That's the only trick you'll lose. Of course, a low trump lead spoils the entries for you, but you're not likely to get that, and you didn't."

The chief was not convinced but acquiesced. "Sorry, I didn't see it."

"Dummy reversals are hard to see — even top experts sometimes have a blind spot with them."

"That makes me feel a little better. By the way, you should drop into headquarters. We have a couple of active cases that might interest you. I may be tied up in meetings, but Lieutenant Morgan can fill you in anyway."

I suffered through the rest of the session.

I arrived at police HQ promptly at one o'clock to find the lieutenant waiting for me. We walked back to her office, but as I sat down, the desk sergeant stuck his head in the door.

"This Hutton woman seems terribly upset, Lieutenant," he said. "Crying fit to bust about her missing husband and she doesn't even know we've found a body. I don't know whether she's in any shape to be questioned."

"Well, try to get her to pull herself together," the lieutenant said impatiently. "Sorry about this, Mr. Bird, I'm going to have to deal with it," Morgan added to me. "A woman came in to report her husband missing after going swimming. As a matter of fact we've already got a body that's probably his, but she doesn't know that. I'm afraid she'll get hysterical when we tell her. Do you want to wait until I'm done with her?"

"No, I'll slide out," I said. "I can come back later if that —"

I broke off. The sergeant had returned already with his charge. Having no wish to intrude on the woman's grief, I paused to let them pass. Then I caught sight of the woman's face and, after a moment of indecision, returned unobtrusively to my chair. She was given a seat facing the lieutenant's desk. She had pulled herself together bravely, but from the clenched hands on her lap it was clear she was vibrating with nerves.

Morgan made soothing noises. "Now, Mrs. Hutton, let me see ... you're worried about your husband?"

The woman nodded, choked, and said, "Yes. He went out for a swim this morning. I was to join him later. His clothes were on the beach, but ... oh, I'm sure ... I'm sure..."

"Take a minute if you need it," said the lieutenant, and then she asked for further details.

These took some time to obtain but amounted to little. Her husband, Mr. Edward Hutton, described as the CEO of a supermarket chain with an office in Toronto and a home in Oakville, had been vacationing with his wife in a luxury condo on the waterfront. He had left their apartment at about ten-thirty that morning, telling his wife he was going to the beach. Mrs. Hutton had planned to join him about noon, but when she arrived there was no sign of her husband, though his clothes were neatly stashed beside a large rock. Mrs. Hutton had called and searched, and then returned to the condo. At that point, being now thoroughly worried, she had decided to report him to the police as a missing person.

The lieutenant nodded. "All right. Now can you give us a description of your husband?"

Mrs. Hutton leaned back in her chair and closed her eyes. "He's five foot seven — no, eight — inches tall, not very broad, thinnish arms and legs, thirty-four inches chest measurement, rather long hands and feet, medium-brown hair, clean-shaven, gray-green eyes and rather a pale complexion; he has an old appendicitis scar, and ... oh, yes, there is a big mole under his left shoulder-blade."

The lieutenant could not restrain her admiration. "Very impressive, Mrs. Hutton. We don't often get that much detail."

"I ... I was thinking about it on the way over here," the woman said faintly. "And here is his passport. I knew you'd want a description."

"Yes. Well ..." Surreptitiously, the lieutenant studied the description of the body now in the mortuary. As I found out later, it tallied in every particular.

With much sympathy, she proceeded to the distasteful task of warning Mrs. Hutton to prepare for a shock. She was afraid that in the mortuary now — if Mrs. Hutton would come along for just a moment... She sighed as the woman gave every sign of imminent hysterics.

"He's here already? Do I have to see him? Must I? Won't ... won't the description be enough?"

It took another twenty minutes to get her into the mortuary to identify the body. But once there she regained her calm. A curious dead-alive look came into her face as the lieutenant gently withdrew the sheet that covered the dead man's face.

"Yes," Mrs. Hutton whispered tonelessly. "That's my husband. That's ... Eddie."

And then I noticed a very curious thing. Like the others, my gaze had been fixed on the sheeted figure on the slab; but when I glanced at Mrs. Hutton, I saw that her eyes were tightly closed. For all she knew, she could have been identifying a piece of cheese as her husband. I nudged the lieutenant.

The lieutenant understood and nodded back. "I'm afraid," she said, as gently as she could, "you must *look* at him, you know."

Mrs. Hutton started violently, opened her eyes, looked at the dead man in front of her, and uttered a horrible, hoarse scream.

For a moment I thought she was going into hysterics again. I jumped forward, as did both the lieutenant and the sergeant, and between them they hurried Mrs. Hutton back to the office. The sergeant produced a glass of water, and within a few minutes the lady was able to stop sobbing and assure them that she was all right, it was just the shock of seeing her own husband, actually lying there...

When at last Mrs. Hutton put down her Kleenex, all three of us heaved sighs of relief. Having at least solved a problem that had been worrying me ever since I first saw Mrs. Hutton in the doorway, I deemed it a good moment to introduce myself.

"Do you know that we've met before, Mrs. Hutton?" I said.

She looked at me vaguely. "No. Have we? Where?"

"At the Toronto Nationals about two years ago. I've been wondering why your face seemed familiar to me. Now I remember. It was at an after-session party, soon after the beginning of the tournament. Do you remember? By the way, have you seen Frank Banditti lately?"

Mrs. Hutton jumped to her feet, her face white. For a moment she gazed wildly at me; then she collapsed on the floor in a dead faint.

"Geez, now look what you did," said the lieutenant reproachfully, as we watched Mrs. Hutton being tidied away into the care of a female police officer. "I thought we'd finally got her calmed down, and then you go and do that."

"I didn't do anything," I said indignantly. "I only reminded her of a party we'd both been to and asked after an old friend of hers. Do you faint when people ask after your old friends?"

"You obviously upset her."

"Apparently. I might try to upset you, too. I might tell you, for instance, that the last time I saw Mrs. Hutton she couldn't tell me whether her husband was a tall man or a short one. Yet now she knows not only his height to an inch but his chest measurement too."

The lieutenant frowned. "What exactly are you suggesting?"

I laughed. "Oh, I'm not suggesting anything. I'm merely pointing out an odd little discrepancy, and you can do what you like with it. But you know," I added thoughtfully, "I would like to have another look at the body, if you've no objection."

"None. But you won't find anything. The medical examiner's had a quick look already, and he definitely drowned. Still, go ahead if you want."

I did not have the mortuary to myself. There were two other men already there. The sergeant, who'd been appointed my conductor, indicated that they were the medical examiner, Dr. Roberts, and Detective Garcia from the Homicide Division. He introduced me, mentioned my acquaintance with the chief, and left me with them. The sheet had been withdrawn from the body and both men were standing by the slab, gazing down. I joined them.

"Pasty-faced guy, eh?" remarked the detective cheerfully. "Certainly no advertisement for our summer sunshine."

I assented absently. I was remembering more and more. *Mr. Banditti says...* Yes, and the husband was to have been a pompous, paunchy little bully, who wouldn't take his wife to tournaments and wouldn't let her go by herself. Well, here I was face to face with the husband at last; he certainly wasn't paunchy and could hardly have been pompous. But that wasn't to say that he might not have been a bully, I thought, looking at the rather weak face and the indeterminate chin: the kind of person that bullies out of weakness instead of strength. Perhaps he was even that pathetic type, the artist *manque* (his hands seemed to indicate the *possibility*) — yes, *manque*, and condemned to an office on Bay Street, and in consequence soured.

"Notice anything, Mr. Bird?" the detective asked eagerly.

I laughed. "Afraid not, this time. Except that Mr. Hutton wasn't as spruce as he might have been."

"How do you make that out, sir?"

"He hadn't shaved this morning."

"Sorry, but he had," the doctor corrected with a smile. "That cut's fresh, at the side of his mouth."

"Well, he needed a new blade," I said feebly.

"Like most of us," the doctor agreed. "But if you're really looking for strange details, what do you make of his back?"

He signed to Garcia, and the two of them turned the corpse over. I saw that the skin on the back was badly lacerated, from the shoulders to the small of the back, and the elbows were almost raw.

"Barnacles?" I suggested.

The doctor nodded. "The rocks on that piece of beach are covered with them. And it was among the rocks that the body was found. Still…"

"I see what you mean. If the body was washing about, why was it lacerated only in that particular area?"

"Yes, it's odd, isn't it? No doubt there's some simple explanation. Perhaps the man who found him pulled him in by the legs."

"No, Doctor," put in the detective. "The body was wedged under a big rock at the side of a pool of water by the shore. Our guys picked him up straight from the ocean."

"There's an abrasion on the front of the right thigh, where he was wedged," supplemented the doctor.

"Yes, but that's natural," I said. "Those scratches aren't."

"And here's another thing. I think those lacerations were made when he was alive. There were signs of bleeding."

"Very interesting," I commented. "Very strange."

"Don't think there's anything wrong, do you?" asked the detective hopefully.

My reply was lost in the sudden return of Lieutenant Morgan.

"Well, looks like we've caught a thief," she announced, not without triumph. "Just had a call from the Mounties in Canada. Seems this fellow was wanted for stock fraud. They've got a warrant out for him, and they'd just heard he'd been seen in this vicinity."

I stared down at the dead man. "You never know, do you? Still, that weak chin..."

"Well, Doctor," the lieutenant continued, "this is bound to open up the possibility that his death wasn't an accident. Any chance, do you think?"

"I'll know more after I've done the post, but there's nothing really obvious at the moment."

"Are you going to check up on Mrs. Hutton's statement, Lieutenant?" I asked suddenly.

Morgan stared. "Yeah, we'll check out her story, of course. Any reason in particular, Mr. Bird?"

"I only wondered," I said mildly. "It would be interesting, for instance, to know if she took a swimsuit with her this morning, wouldn't it? Or if she left the house soon after her husband, and not at noon?"

"I guess," said Garcia, whose job it would be to make these inquiries. "You don't think...?"

"I only think it might be interesting," I replied.

As I trudged along the coarse sand the next day, I wondered if I was wasting my time and energy. I was convinced that Hutton had been murdered, and the method was fairly obvious. But could the woman have done it? Physically, yes. But psychologically? Hardly. She was too vague, too woolly, too ... silly.

Did silliness mean one couldn't commit murder? Murder itself was usually very silly. Mrs. Hutton might not be the stuff of which strong, silent murderers were made, but mightn't she be a silly murderess? She was a hero-worshipper. How far would hero-worship carry her?

My plodding feet seemed to be picking out a shambling refrain. *Banditti ... Mr. Banditti says...* And suppose Mr. Banditti had said, "Pick up your husband's feet when he's bathing and hold them up in the air for a few minutes, and then I shall be able to marry you and your millions."

Oh, Mr. Banditti was in it, all right. Why else faint at the mere mention of his name? And of course there was other evidence of guilt. First, she wouldn't look at the body at all; then, when she was made to, took one peek, turned green, and screamed. If that wasn't presumptive evidence of guilt, what was?

And reeling off the description in that way! I could almost hear the voice of her tutor: "If they wonder how you've got it so pat, just say you were thinking it out on the way, or remembered it from his passport or something. They won't question that." And pat she certainly had got it, like a child repeating a lesson. But Mr. Banditti should have devoted more time to his artistic effects.

I looked along the beach ahead of me and saw Detective Garcia clambering over a pile of rocks. This must be the place.

"I'm really just going through the motions here," he greeted me. "It looks like a pretty straightforward accident, but I know you've got some idea about it being a murder."

"I never mentioned the word," I protested.

"No, but it was obvious what you thought. I agree there seems to be something fishy about Mrs. Hutton. More I think of it, more it seems to me that she was putting on an act."

"Have you been over to their condo?"

"Yeah. Hell of a fancy place on the water, with a marina, golf, tennis, the whole shooting match. Must have cost them a packet. And they've got a live-in maid, which was handy for me. They've got money to burn all right, those Huttons. Still, her story checks out so far as it goes. She did leave at the time she said, and she didn't take a swimsuit."

"Any signs of ... worry?"

"No!" said the detective emphatically. "I asked that specially, and the maid said she seemed just as usual before she went out. Hadn't got into a fight with her husband or anything. But when she came back! Tears? Floods of 'em. And before he'd been missing long enough to make any ordinary wife even start worrying."

"Mmm ... remorse? I wonder." I was a little puzzled. Banditti would surely be too shrewd to spring an unexpected murder on a foolish, possibly unreliable woman. I pushed the point aside. "Anyhow, where was he found?"

The detective pointed out the spot. The tide had gone down far enough for me, balanced precariously on the slippery surface, to be able to inspect the crevice in which the body had been wedged. It told me nothing.

He gazed thoughtfully over the shore. "Well, I think I'd like another word or two with the guy who found the body. You never know. He might have noticed something."

"Good idea," I agreed. "I'll poke round here for a bit if you want to pick me up on your way back."

It didn't take me long to turn up something. In the third pool I explored, shining merrily only a few inches below the surface, was a gold ring, just asking to be found. Scarcely able to believe my luck, I examined it. It was a man's wedding ring, and the inside was inscribed "E. H. B. G. 18 November, 1982."

I slowly turned it over in my hand. It was a chance in a million. And yet what did it prove? That Edward Hutton had died in that particular pool. Not very much.

I put my shoes and socks back on and sat down to wait for Garcia to return.

He came bursting with news. "She's in it all right, Mr. Bird. We found a man who was beachcombing yesterday afternoon. He says he saw a woman here about three o'clock, and the description of the clothes tallies near enough."

"Mrs. Hutton didn't mention being on the beach then?"

"No, she did not. But that's not all. There was a man there, too."

"Yes, there would be."

"You expected that?" asked the detective, a trifle disappointed.

"In a way. Well, what did they do?"

"They came out of a little cave here. After a minute or two, the man went back into the cave and the woman went off along the beach."

"Did you get any description of the man?"

"Nothing particular. Orange sweatshirt, grey pants. Clean-shaven."

"Clean-shaven, eh? Yes, well, that fits."

"Sorry?"

"He had a beard last time I saw him, but beards are much too distinctive. Detective, it's time I told you a few things. Let's sit down."

We made ourselves comfortable on the sand, and I told my tale.

"Mind you," I concluded, "there's no evidence that the man's Banditti. After all, it was over two years ago and she may have a new hero by now. But it's worth a few inquiries."

"No question. What do you think I should do?"

"Well, if it were me, I would really want to ask Mrs. Hutton why she fainted at Banditti's name."

But I did not go back with Garcia to hear the answer to this interesting question. Instead, I left Mrs. Hutton in peace and took out my cellphone. My objective was Natalie Dormer in Toronto, and I was lucky enough to catch her at home.

Yes, as far as she knew, the link between Frank Banditti and his groceress had survived the tournament trail to date. He was on to a good thing there, and it wasn't likely he'd let it go. No, he hadn't been caught courting some new client; oh, yes, a faithful partner, naturally.

"Would you say that Banditti was unscrupulous?" I asked carefully.

"You mean, would he cheat if it was going to get him a win bonus or—" Natalie began.

"No, no. Worse than that. Stop at absolutely nothing, I mean."

Natalie's keen nose scented gossip, and we discussed the possibilities. In the end, her view was that Mr. Banditti was probably unscrupulous enough for murder if driven to it, but it wouldn't be *like* him.

"I see," I said thoughtfully. "Then I wonder what did drive him. Something big, presumably. Money troubles, maybe? They can be big enough, for sure. But what drove *her*? She doesn't look unscrupulous at all. It must have been something even bigger. Love, I suppose. You know, there's something really odd about this case, Natalie."

"Why do you assume Mrs. Hutton was driven at all?" Natalie asked. "You say she was perfectly normal that morning. A woman of her type couldn't appear normal with her husband's murder imminent."

"No, you're right. In fact, she may not know it was murder, even now. Why shouldn't Mr. Banditti have said it was an accident and that she must just keep his name out of it for convenience? Yes! That explains her part much better. Yet ... that excessive grief, for a husband she couldn't have loved? I don't know. No, it still doesn't fit, somehow. I think I'll take a walk."

What I needed now were a couple of nice, juicy coincidences. I got one at the tournament the following morning, when I ran into Mrs. Hutton by the bookstand.

Mrs. Hutton seemed not exactly overjoyed to see me, but told me that she thought playing bridge might take her mind off her situation. I was officiously helpful and insisted on escorting her to the desk where they were selling entries for the day's main event.

But I learned little. The place was too crowded to allow intimate conversation, and Mrs. Hutton was obviously far too scared of me to respond even had we been alone. I listened to a pair filling out a convention card.

"I always bypass diamonds, whatever my hand strength. Mr. Fantoni says…"

The rhythm was familiar. Mister Banditti says, Mister Banditti says… *You don't need to look at him when you identify him. Just keep your eyes closed and say it's your husband. They won't notice.* Had Mr. Banditti said that?

But why not look at an unloved husband, so sadly and accidentally drowned? Is one so frightened that one cannot look at him? No, it didn't fit. Mrs. Hutton must have some guilty knowledge, even if she wasn't involved in the murder itself.

I looked at the faded, once-pretty face. Mrs. Hutton caught me at it, started violently, blushed unnecessarily, and looked away.

Wow, I thought, the woman's as nervous as a kitten. Why?

By the time the session started, I still had no answer. During the dinner break, I decided to stop by police HQ once again and see if there had been any developments.

If I felt that I had little to show for two days' work, that was certainly not the case with Detective Garcia. Almost before I had time to ask for a cup of coffee, he burst into his story.

"You were right, Mr. Bird. We've found Banditti. Well, got on his track, at least. He was camping on the beach, not a mile from the crime scene."

"Ah," I said, and noted that now it was officially a crime.

"And about one-thirty — that's a good couple of hours after the murder, by our reckoning — he was seen taking his tent down by a woman out jogging. Then he bolted. Packed his tent and things, all lightweight stuff, on to his motorcycle, and rode straight off.

"Now here's something else. When the jogger saw him, he still had a beard. When he was seen around three o'clock, by the beachcomber, he had shaved it off."

"Ah," I said again. "Yes, that's interesting. Are you sure of that?"

"Absolutely. The jogger ran past him not fifty yards away. She says she could see Banditti quite plainly."

"How was he dressed?"

"The same. Sweatshirt and grey pants."

"Have you found any trace of the tent or motorcycle?"

"None. He must have hidden them before he doubled back to meet Mrs. Hutton, and afterwards he picked them up and took off. We've put out an APB for him."

"Quick work. Now here's another point. I take it that your times are correct? What time does the doctor say that death occurred?"

"About eleven o'clock, he thinks. Anyhow, between ten and one. He was dead when Banditti took down his tent, if that's what you're getting at."

"Yes, partly. And when he was taking down his tent, at one-thirty, Banditti had his beard. Less than two hours after, he hadn't. Well, here's my point. How did Banditti get hold of a razor? Men with beards don't carry them."

Garcia frowned. "That hadn't occurred to me."

"Well, if he did have a razor with him, wouldn't that show that the murder was premeditated? If he didn't, it was probably done on the spur of the moment."

"Well, he didn't," said Garcia. "He got hold of one, and I can tell you where he got it from. Look at this list."

I looked. The paper contained a minute inventory of the belongings of the late Mr. Hutton, as left in his apartment. It was complete down to extra toothpaste. I ran my eye quickly down the column. An old-fashioned shaving brush was listed, along with shaving soap, but there was no razor.

"Interesting. So Mrs. Hutton took it to him at three o'clock?"

"That's when she met him for the second time," said the detective.

"The second time? Oh, I see. You mean, she met him first at twelve, and took instructions. Yes, of course." I drank my coffee. "Well, that certainly seems to wrap it up. So all you've got to do now is to find Banditti."

"Yes, and Mrs. Hutton too," said Garcia, not without resentment. "She gave us the slip yesterday. Went to meet Banditti, I'll bet. We'll pick her up again all right, but she may have tipped him off that — oh, hi, Lieutenant!"

"Ah! Mr. Bird, there you are again!" said Morgan genially, poking her head into Garcia's cubicle. "Well, it looks as though you were right. And now we've got both you and Mrs. Hutton here again. We picked her up at the airport."

Garcia grinned. "It's time we asked Mrs. Hutton a few questions."

"Agreed. She's in Interview Room 1. You're welcome to come, Mr. Bird. You were in at the beginning, so you may as well see the end."

In less than two minutes, Mrs. Hutton was once again seated opposite the lieutenant; but this time we had a frankly terrified woman and a police official who no longer spoke to her kindly. I watched Mrs. Hutton waiting like a cornered mouse for the spring of the cat, and felt rather sick. She was such a silly woman. Who but a woman of almost sublime silliness would bring her lover a razor with which to shave off his beard, but omit to bring the shaving soap?

And suddenly something in my brain went *click* and I saw the whole thing. I glanced quickly from the lieutenant to the detective, calculating my chances. No, there was not a second to lose. In another moment, they might ruin the whole thing. I would have to charge in and brave the wrath that would certainly come after.

"Lieutenant, may I ask Mrs. Hutton just one question first?"

Morgan looked surprised but gave permission. I moved my chair so that I could look at the woman more directly. "Mrs. Hutton, do you mind telling me this: Are you sure you really know what happened on the beach that morning?"

Mrs. Hutton's jaw dropped. Obviously she had not expected the question; equally obviously, she did not know how to answer it.

I followed it quickly with another. "Do you know, for instance, that *murder* was committed?"

Mrs. Hutton started to her feet, prepared to scream, thought better of it, and fainted.

"That's enough! I don't care if you do play bridge with the chief – you'd better have a good explanation for this!" exclaimed Morgan, in real anger.

Once more, Mrs. Hutton was borne unconscious into the back regions.

"Listen, Lieutenant!" I pleaded. "The whole point was that Mrs. Hutton never knew that there had been a murder. If you'd broken it gently, you'd have given her time to adjust herself to the idea, and she might have decided to help cover it up. Now she's had a bad shock — and she'll talk!

"We've been making a mistake from the beginning," I continued urgently. "A fundamental mistake. I've only just realized it. You see, this murder *was* planned. A long time ago, I bet. A pit was carefully dug for us and we fell into it. At first sight, it looks a terrific gamble and yet ... police procedure is so rigid. Yes, that's the clue: police procedure is so rigid. Your own procedure protected the murderer. He'd banked on it.

"It was clever," I continued musingly. "He killed two birds with one stone. That warrant for Hutton's arrest ... he must've got wind of it somehow. By the way, did Hutton have a big life insurance policy? I think you'll find he did. Yes, of course he must have had. That's another thing Mrs. Hutton was intended to do: collect the insurance money. That was to be a tidy windfall for him to cash in on, even if everything else went down the tubes.

"Of course, the swim was carefully arranged. Right time, right place, deserted beach, and all the rest. And then ... up with his heels in some convenient pool, and what does it matter if his back gets scratched on the barnacles so long as his head stays under water? Nothing simpler! Then wedge the body where with any luck it won't drift loose for a few tides, and even if it does, what are the odds?

"Mrs. Hutton, of course, knew nothing in advance. That puzzled me from the start. How could such a foolish woman be trusted with murder plans? Obviously she couldn't. And naturally, when she met him on the beach, he told her it was an accident. But what a convenient accident! It could be made to fit right in with their own plans. So he told her the tale about the warrant and everything, and how the authorities would probably seize all their assets except the insurance money, and why he must be kept out of it all, and what she must do. I expect he had some difficulty in rehearsing her, owing to floods of tears; that's why he didn't emphasize the importance of details as he should have done. So of course she managed to give things away. She would. That was the one flaw in his plan, having to rely on poor Mrs. Hutton. But he had no choice.

"So that was that. And if things went right, there was his future all nicely secured, and his hated rival out of the way! Yes, I think he was actually jealous. He must have been fond of Mrs. Hutton in his own way. After all, she suited him very well. Anyhow, he couldn't stand having a rival in her regard, so ... exit rival! Hence those tears. She was fond of the rival, you see. Much too fond, in his opinion.

"Now shall I tell you what suddenly gave it away to me? It was that shaving-brush and soap. How like Mrs. Hutton, I thought, to take her lover a razor to shave off his beard and not take the shaving soap; and I wondered if even Mrs. Hutton could have been so silly. Well, of course she wasn't. The shaving soap wasn't taken because soap doesn't lather in seawater, so it would be no use. Ridiculous little point for such a case to hang on, isn't it? But the case does hang on it. Because Mrs. Hutton wouldn't know a thing like that. So it wasn't she who left the shaving soap behind, and so it wasn't she who took the razor—"

"Who did take the razor?" interrupted the lieutenant.

"The murderer, of course! Just as he brought that false beard to Florida with him, probably bought months ago. By the way, how delighted he must have been with that orange sweatshirt. You see, any bearded face surmounting an orange sweatshirt is just the same at fifty yards as any other bearded face surmounting—"

"Wait a minute," Morgan looked bewildered. "False beards? Orange sweatshirts? What are you getting at?"

"I mean," I said gently, "that you shouldn't have relied on Mrs. Hutton's sole identification of her husband's body. You see, the body you've got in that mortuary isn't Edward Hutton. It's Frank Banditti."

An older gentleman had been sitting quietly at the edge of our group, watching and listening attentively to Bird's tale and its predecessors. He was clearly able to follow the bridge narratives, so I invited him to introduce himself and contribute to the evening's enjoyment.

"Yes, well," he began, "I'm Bill Miller. I never actually play bridge, but I enjoy attending tournaments and competitions and watching the great players perform at the table. My favorite is Professor Silver, whose exploits are always entertaining and sometimes exciting. For example, during the last Nationals..."

6

THE KIBITZER'S TALE

In the opening rounds of the Spingold, I was kibitzing the great professor when two scruffy looking opponents arrived at his table. They introduced themselves as David Hume and George Berkeley, members of a British team from Oxford University. A hand came up, a fairly routine contract without any drama, but what was interesting was the postmortem that followed. It was the last board of the match. Neither team appeared to have much of an advantage, and this last hand seemed destined to be a push.

Wright Cardinal
♠ 8 4 2
♡ Q 4
◇ 8 6 5
♣ Q 10 9 4 2

Berkeley
♠ Q 10 9 7
♡ 8 6 3 2
◇ Q J 10
♣ K 6

	N	
W		E
	S	

Hume
♠ —
♡ 9 7 5
◇ 9 4 3 2
♣ A J 8 7 5 3

Professor Silver
♠ A K J 6 5 3
♡ A K J 10
◇ A K 7
♣ —

Professor Silver opened the bidding with a strong 2♣ bid and a scientific, exploratory auction ensued.

West	North	East	South
George	Wright	David	Professor
Berkeley	Cardinal	Hume	Silver
	pass	pass	2♣
pass	2◇	pass	2♠
pass	4♠	pass	6♡
pass	6♠	all pass	

The opening lead was the ◇Q. Professor Silver won the ◇A and cashed the ♠A, getting the bad news when RHO showed out. He played out the ♡AKJ, discarding a diamond from dummy. This was followed by the ◇K and a diamond ruff in dummy. He then conceded one down, as there were two inescapable trump losers.

"Sorry, Wright," he said amiably, "the 4-0 spade split doomed the contract. There were only eleven tricks to be had as the cards lie."

"Actually, there is no such a thing as a trick," Berkeley interjected.

"I beg your pardon? How can you say that? Of course there is such a thing as a trick!" retorted Professor Silver.

"Since we have time now, let me give you an analogy," replied Berkeley. "When I read a book, what I actually see are the letters on the page; but the letters make words, and these suggest ideas. They could be notions of God, virtue, truth, etcetera. Now, obviously the letters are perceived by my senses — they are 'sensible', so to speak. But are the things suggested by them also 'sensible'?"

"Of course not, it would be absurd. Abstract ideas remain abstract, even though they may be suggested to the mind by marks on paper with which they have an arbitrary connection," replied Professor Silver dismissively.

"Well, in the same way, some bridge players imagine they can look at their hand and dummy and see tricks. Of course, this is an optimistic delusion. When you look at the cards, you have an experience that has a connection with the physical cards, a connection proceeding through photons, rods and cones, and the optic nerve to the brain. All these stages are necessary if you are to have the visual experience that's called 'seeing the tricks.' When a bridge player 'looks' at the hands, there's a connection with the tricks he thinks he's seeing, but that doesn't make them real or guarantee that he will take them," Berkeley pursued.

"But are you seriously suggesting that nothing is real? Suppose you want to write down the result on this hand — wouldn't you use a pen and a scorecard, like anyone else? And don't you know what they are?" asked the Professor incredulously.

"Professor, let me emphasize again: I don't know the real nature of anything in the universe. I may use a pen and a scorecard. But what either of them really is, I have no idea. What is more, I cannot prove that they even exist. We certainly perceive objects or ideas, such as tricks, but it cannot be concluded as a result that tricks really exist." Berkeley smiled.

"I assure you, Berkeley, I am a simple man, simple enough to believe my senses and leave things as I find them. If I can see it, it's real," said Professor Silver.

"But Professor," interjected Hume, "how many times have you doubled a contract because you 'held' sufficient tricks to beat it, only to find when you led an ace that declarer ruffed it, and that the 'trick' that you perceived a moment ago was actually in declarer's hand in the form of a small trump?"

"Perhaps you are confusing cards with tricks?" said Berkeley. "The cards are certainly things we feel and see, but they contain information. In the case of your ace, its rank and suit. The ace is an object whose trick-taking properties are known, so you don't doubt that it's exactly what it seems to be, a trick. Similarly, a low-ranking spotcard, if it is in the company of several higher-ranking cards of the same suit, will be seen as a potential trick, since its more powerful brethren may extract all extant cards of that suit and allow it to become a winner. But what if the higher-ranking cards are not sufficient to clear the suit, and the low-ranking spotcard loses the trick to a slightly higher-ranking spotcard? If you held a solid five-card suit, would you double three notrump if you weren't on lead? Of course not, for declarer might cash nine or ten tricks without touching your strong suit. Your potential tricks vanish if you can't declare your suit as trumps or lead it during the play.

"We perceive tricks through mental representations of them. These 'tricks' may or may not correspond to the physical reality, as, for example, Professor, in your mishandling of the slam you just played."

"Be careful, young man," advised Wright Cardinal.

"Mishandling?" snarled Professor Silver.

"It was misplayed!" responded Berkeley, undaunted. "Let's have another look at the hand."

Wright Cardinal
- ♠ 8 4 2
- ♡ Q 4
- ♢ 8 6 5
- ♣ Q 10 9 4 2

Berkeley
- ♠ Q 10 9 7
- ♡ 8 6 3 2
- ♢ Q J 10
- ♣ K 6

	N	
W		E
	S	

Hume
- ♠ —
- ♡ 9 7 5
- ♢ 9 4 3 2
- ♣ A J 8 7 5 3

Professor Silver
- ♠ A K J 6 5 3
- ♡ A K J 10
- ♢ A K 7
- ♣ —

"Just because you can perceive only eleven tricks does not mean there isn't another one available. You simply have to transfer one of West's two trump tricks to your hand. Since you can't literally retrieve a card from his grasp, you have to engineer an endplay to make your contract. His second trump trick is only *potentially* his, and you need him to be on lead in the endgame. But you need his physical cards to conform to a particular distribution so you assume that he is 4=4=3=2 and play accordingly.

"You win the opening diamond lead and lay down the ace of spades. Then you follow with the ace and jack of hearts, winning with dummy's queen. Ruff a club and cash the heart king, discarding a diamond from dummy. Then the king of diamonds and a diamond ruff in dummy is followed by another club ruff in your hand. The ten of hearts is now tabled, as West follows and you ruff in dummy. Now everyone is down to three cards, so you play a club from dummy and ruff it with the three. West must overruff and lead from his queen-ten of spades into your king-jack. So you see, West's second trump trick didn't exist in his hand but in yours, Professor."

"But the trick did exist," blurted Professor Silver. "All you've done is change its location."

"Not so," returned Berkeley. "What you call 'tricks' are merely the arbitrary result of placing cards on the table, and abiding by the rules of a game we call 'bridge.' The same card can win for declarer or defender, depending on the presence or absence of a trump suit or even, as we've just seen, on which player initiates the play. The result of your so-called trick is completely situational and isn't contained in an attribute called 'a trick.'"

"Enough, gentlemen," said Wright Cardinal. "I can end this argument quite simply. Tricks must exist — or how would Professor Silver be able to make so many of them disappear?"

It was getting late, and we all still had a long way to drive the next day. But the coffee urn was not empty, and none of us showed much inclination to head up to our rooms. There was a pause after the previous narrative, and I wondered if we had finally run out of strange stories. But no — a distinguished-looking older man leaned forward.

"Are any of you familiar with the St. Clair Bridge Club?" he inquired. "No? Well, not surprising, I suppose. I happened to be privy to a very strange evening that took place within its walls not so very long ago. Would you like to hear about it?"

There was a general murmur of assent, and he began…

7

THE BRIDGE CLUB MEMBER'S TALE

The St. Clair Bridge Club is the most difficult club in the world to join. Being accepted into it distinguishes the new member more than if he had won a world title or been elected to the Hall of Fame. Those who belong to the St. Clair Bridge Club never mention that fact. If you ask one of them which club he plays at, he will name all but that particular one. He is afraid that if he told you he belonged to the St. Clair, it would seem like boasting.

The St. Clair originally stood on the present site of the Royal York Hotel. It has a whist trophy, which Queen Victoria presented to the club, and houses the original manuscript of the *Contract Bridge Blue Book*, bequeathed to it by Ely Culbertson himself. When they write letters or notes at the club, the members still use pen and paper — no modern technology is allowed inside.

The St. Clair enjoys the distinction of having, without political prejudice, blackballed an ex-prime minister of each party. At the same sitting, it elected Laskin, the Supreme Court Justice, who was at the time a penniless young lawyer, to membership.

When Paul Preval, the French artist who came to Toronto to paint the portrait of the Ontario premier, was made a member (foreigners are only honorary members), he said, "I would rather see my name on the list here than on a picture in the Louvre." At which Curly, who oversaw the card tables, remarked, "That is not such a compliment, because men who have works in the Louvre have been dead fifty years."

The St. Clair has only one room to the club and many card tables; each card table boasts an overhead light, but the dining area, as has been the case since the club began, is illuminated only by candles.

The night after the great fog of 2013, there were five members present — four of them busy with supper and one reading in front of the fireplace. The four men at the table were strangers to one another, but as they picked at their desserts and sipped their coffee, they conversed with such animation that a visitor to the club — which does not tolerate visitors — would have assumed them to be good friends. But it is the etiquette and tradition of the St. Clair that everyone must speak with anyone there. There is but one long table, and whether there are twenty at it or two, the waiters, supporting the rule, will place them side by side. For this reason, the four strangers were seated together at their meal, the long cover of the table cutting a green path through the outer gloom of the room.

"I repeat," said the gentleman with the pink plaid shirt, "that the days for romantic adventure have passed, and that the fault lies with us. I do not regard sectionals as adventures. Even that fellow Chetney, who turned up this week at the Nationals when everyone thought he had died in South Africa, did nothing remarkable over there. He beat up the local *patzers* and won a twelve-table Open Pairs at some small Regional. No, one no longer ventures. We are grown too practical — above all, too sensible. We have here, in the persons of Professor Silver and myself, an illustration of how ways have changed."

The men around the table turned and glanced toward the gentleman in front of the fireplace. He was an elderly and somewhat portly person, with a kindly wrinkled countenance that wore a smile of almost childish confidence and good nature. It was a face that the media and Internet had made intimately familiar. He held a book from him at arm's length, as though to adjust it to his eyesight, and his brows were knit with concentration.

"Now, were we living in more adventurous times," continued the gentleman in the pink shirt, "when Professor Silver left the club this afternoon I would have had him bound and gagged and thrown into a taxi. My hired ruffians would convey him to some lonely spot where they would guard him until midnight. Nothing would come of it, except a boost in my reputation as a gentleman of adventurous spirit, and an article in the *Globe and Mail,* with stars for names, entitled, perhaps, 'The Professor and the Bridge Player.'"

"But why?" inquired the youngest of the members. "And Professor Silver — why select him in particular for this adventure?"

The gentleman with the pink shirt shrugged his shoulders. "It would prevent him from playing in the evening session of the Spingold. My team is tied with his at the half," he added gloomily, "and if he plays tonight, we'll easily lose."

All the gentlemen again turned and surveyed the Professor with freshened interest. The honorary member of the club, whose accent had already betrayed him as an American, laughed softly.

"He hasn't lifted his eyes from that book since we first came in."

The others nodded.

"Surely, he's not intending to play tonight," added the youngest member.

"Oh, yes, he will play," muttered the man in the pink shirt moodily. "At game time, he'll be in his place and they will undoubtedly win the match."

The fourth member, a stout and florid gentleman in a short smoking jacket and black tie, sighed enviously.

"Fancy one of us being as cool as that," he said, "if he knew he had to play one of the top Canadian teams tonight. I certainly wouldn't be. And yet he's as relaxed over that book as though he had nothing else to do until bedtime."

"Yes, see how focused he is," whispered the youngest member. "It's probably some abstruse collection of double-dummy problems."

The gentleman with the pink shirt laughed morosely. "The abstruse work in which our eminent expert is so deeply engrossed," he said, "is called *The Great Fog Robbery*. It's a detective novel currently on the bestseller list."

The American raised his eyebrows in disbelief. "*The Great Fog Robbery*?" he repeated incredulously. "What an odd choice!"

"It's his vice," returned the gentleman with the pink shirt. "It's his one weakness. He's noted for it. Professor Silver seeks relaxation in detective stories. He brings these wretched little paperbacks even into this club and reads them at the table while he's dummy. Once he's started on a tale of murder, robbery, and mayhem, nothing can tear him from it."

The member twisted his shirt sleeve nervously and bit at the edge of his mustache. "If only it were the first pages of that novel he was reading," he murmured bitterly, "instead of the last! With such a prospect before him, I swear he would be here until the club closes. There would be no need of anything else to keep him from the Spingold."

The eyes of all were fastened upon Professor Silver, and they saw with fascination that with his forefinger he was now separating the last two pages of the book. The member struck the table softly with his open palm.

"I would give a hundred dollars," he whispered, "if I could place in his hands at this moment a new edition of *The Maltese Falcon* — a thousand," he added wildly. "Five thousand dollars!"

The American observed the speaker sharply, as though the words had some special application to him, and then, at a thought that had apparently just struck him, smiled to himself.

Professor Silver ceased reading but, as though still under the influence of the book, sat looking blankly into the open fire. For a brief space, no one moved until the Professor, with a sudden start of recollection, looked at his watch. He scanned its face and rose slowly to his feet. The voice of the American instantly broke the silence.

"Perhaps the Professor would settle our dispute over this unfortunate hand that my partner claims I misplayed?"

"Not now, I'll be late for the evening session," Professor Silver demurred.

"Please, Professor, it will take you but a few seconds and greatly oblige us. The hand is right here on the table."

"All right, but just a quick look."

"I was declarer in six diamonds, and they led the queen of clubs."

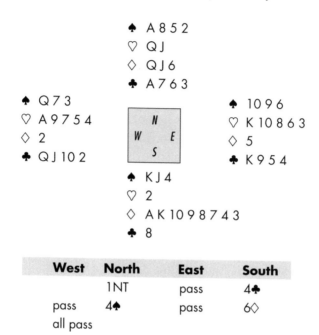

♠ A 8 5 2
♡ Q J
◇ Q J 6
♣ A 7 6 3

♠ Q 7 3
♡ A 9 7 5 4
◇ 2
♣ Q J 10 2

♠ 10 9 6
♡ K 10 8 6 3
◇ 5
♣ K 9 5 4

♠ K J 4
♡ 2
◇ A K 10 9 8 7 4 3
♣ 8

West	North	East	South
	1NT	pass	4♣
pass	4♠	pass	6◇
all pass			

"Hmm. Lucky for you they didn't lead a heart, as then you need the spade finesse. Since you went down, I suspect that's what you tried anyway. But there is a better line of play on a club lead. Win with the ace and ruff a club. Travel to the dummy via the trump queen and ruff another club, back to the jack of diamonds to ruff your last club, then play two more rounds of trumps and arrive at this position:

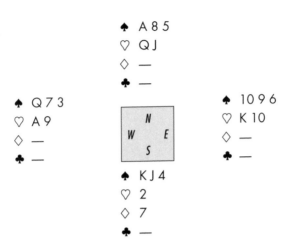

```
              ♠  A 8 5
              ♡  Q J
              ♢  —
              ♣  —
♠  Q 7 3          ┌─────────┐        ♠  10 9 6
♡  A 9            │    N    │        ♡  K 10
♢  —             │ W     E │        ♢  —
♣  —             │    S    │        ♣  —
                  └─────────┘
              ♠  K J 4
              ♡  2
              ♢  7
              ♣  —
```

"Of course, you have figured out the most likely East-West distributions are 3=5=1=4 with split heart honors. Play the last trump. West discards a heart, dummy a spade, and East a spade. Now the cross to dummy with the ♠A and then the ♡Q is the winning play. The location of the ♠Q is irrelevant."

"Brilliant, Professor! You are the Sherlock Holmes of bridge," said the man in the pink shirt.

"True," remarked the American. "But I don't think that Sherlock Holmes himself could decipher the mystery that baffles the police of Toronto tonight."

At these unexpected words, which carried with them something of a challenge, the gentlemen about the table started as suddenly as if the American had fired a pistol in the air, and Professor Silver halted and stood looking at him with grave surprise.

The gentleman with the pink shirt was the first to recover.

"What's this?" he said eagerly, staring across the table. "A mystery baffles the police of Toronto? There's been nothing on the news. Tell us about it."

The American flushed uncomfortably. "Only the police know of it," he murmured, "and they know only because I told them. It's a remarkable crime, and unfortunately I'm the only witness, which is why I'm detained in Toronto." Inclining his head politely, he said, "I'm Sears — Commander Ripley Sears, of the United States Navy — at present naval attaché at the US Embassy in Ottawa. If I wasn't kept here, I'd be on my way to Washington right now."

The gentleman with the pink shirt interrupted with an exclamation of excitement and delight. "Do you hear that, Professor?" he cried jubilantly. "An American diplomat detained by our police because he's the only witness to a crime — a most remarkable crime, I believe you said," he added, bending eagerly toward the naval officer.

The American nodded and glanced at the two other members. Professor Silver advanced to within the light of the candles.

"The crime must be exceptional indeed," he said, "to justify the police preventing you from traveling."

The gentleman with the pink shirt pushed a chair toward Professor Silver and motioned him to be seated.

"You can't leave us now," he exclaimed. "Commander Sears is just about to tell us the details." He nodded vigorously at the American, who after first glancing doubtfully toward the waiters at the far end of the room, leaned forward across the table. The others drew their chairs nearer and bent toward him. The Professor glanced irresolutely at his watch and with an exclamation of annoyance turned back to the group.

"They can wait," he muttered. He seated himself quickly and nodded at Commander Sears. "Please begin," he said impatiently.

"Of course," said the American, "you understand that I'm speaking in confidence. You've heard nothing and you know no one connected with this mystery. Even I must remain anonymous."

The men seated around him nodded gravely.

"Of course," Professor Silver assented with eagerness, "of course."

"We will refer to it," said the gentleman with the pink shirt, "as 'The Story of the Naval Attaché.'"

The American began his story.

"I arrived in Toronto two days ago for meetings at our consulate, and I checked in at the Royal York. Most of my work is in Ottawa, and I don't know many people in Toronto. But a couple of years ago at a bridge tournament in Hong Kong, I'd played with an officer in the Canadian Navy, who has since retired and now lives in a small house in the Annex. I texted him that I was in town and received an invitation to have dinner at his house yesterday evening. He's a bachelor, so we ate alone and swapped bridge stories for the evening. I was leaving the next morning for Washington and had to catch up with some work email, so at about ten o'clock I decided to head back to the hotel. He phoned for a taxi to pick me up, but apparently with no result.

"'They're usually here pretty quickly,' my friend said. He walked to the window, pulled back the curtains. 'Have you ever seen a Toronto fog?' he asked. 'Take a look at this.'

"I joined him at the window, but I could see nothing. If I hadn't known the house looked out on the street, I would've believed I was facing a wall. I opened the window and stuck out my head but could see nothing. Even the street lights had been smothered in the yellow mist. The lights of the room in which I stood penetrated the darkness only to a distance of a few inches from my eyes.

"My friend was still trying to get a taxi on the phone, but I decided that I would head back to the hotel on foot — it wasn't that far. I needed to get back, and, besides, I had always heard that being out in a thick fog was a wonderful experience, and I was curious to experience it for myself.

"My friend went with me to his front door and laid down a course for me to follow. First, I was to walk straight across the street to a brick wall. I was then to feel my way to the left along the wall until I came to a row of houses set back from the sidewalk. They would bring me to a cross street. On the other side of this street was a row of shops that I was to follow until they joined the iron fence that went around the museum. I was to keep to the fence until I reached the gates at City Hall, where I was to cross Queen Street and tack in toward the railings of Osgoode Hall. At the end of these railings, going south, I would find the railway station and my hotel.

"To a sailor, the course did not seem difficult, so I said goodnight and walked forward until I reached the sidewalk. A few steps farther, my hands struck the wall. I turned in the direction from which I had just come and saw a square of faint light cut into the black darkness. I shouted 'All right!' and my friend's voice answered, 'Good luck!' The light from his open door disappeared, and I was left alone in a misty, yellow darkness. I've been in the Navy for twenty years, but I've never known a fog like last night's, not even among the icebergs of the Bering Sea. I couldn't even make out my hand in front of me on the wall. At sea, a fog is a natural phenomenon. But a fog springing from the paved streets, rolling between solid housefronts, forcing cars to move at a crawl and extinguishing the street lights … that's as out of place as a tidal wave in Iowa.

"As I felt my way along the wall, I encountered other people who were coming from the opposite direction, and each time, I stepped away from the wall to make room for them to pass. But the third time I did this, when I reached out my hand, the wall had disappeared, and the farther I moved to find it, the more I had the unpleasant feeling that at any moment I might step over a precipice. Since I'd set out, I'd heard no traffic in the street, and now, although I listened for a while, I could distinguish only the occasional footfalls of pedestrians. Several times I called out, and once, a jocular gentleman answered me, but only to ask me where I thought he was, and then even he was swallowed up in the silence. Just above me I could make out a street light, and I moved over to that and, while I tried to recover my bearings, kept my hand on the iron post. Except for this light, I could see nothing. I could hear occasional sounds, but I couldn't tell where they came from.

"I decided that I'd better remain where I was until someone could help me. I must have waited for ten minutes, straining my ears and hailing distant footfalls. From somewhere near me I heard music, but I couldn't make out where from. There seemed to be no use waiting longer, so I set out again and at once bumped into a low iron fence. Following it, I found that it stretched for a long distance, and that there were gates at regular intervals. I was standing uncertainly, my hand on one of these, when a square of light suddenly opened in the night, and in it I saw, as you see a picture thrown by a projector in a darkened theater, a young gentleman in a tuxedo, and behind him, the lights of a hallway. I decided to approach and ask him to tell me where I was. But while I was fumbling with the latch of the gate, the door closed, leaving only a narrow shaft of light. Whether he had reentered the house or left it, I couldn't tell, but I stepped through the gate and found myself upon an asphalt walk. There was the sound of steps on the path and someone hurried past me. I called to him, but he didn't reply, and I heard the gate click and footsteps hurrying away.

"Under other circumstances, the young man's rudeness, and his recklessness in hurrying through the mist, would have struck me as strange, but everything was so distorted by the fog that I didn't think about it. The door was as he'd left it — partly open. I went up the path and, after much fumbling, found the doorbell and gave it a push. The bell echoed from a great depth and distance, but no movement followed from inside the house, and although I rang and knocked again and again, I heard nothing. I was anxious to be on my way, but I had decided that until I knew where I was I would not venture back into the fog. So I pushed the door open and stepped into the house.

"I found myself in a long and narrow hall with doors along either side. At the end of the hall was a staircase with a balustrade that ended in a sweeping curve. The balustrade was covered with heavy rugs, and the walls of the hall were also hung with them. The door on my left was closed, but the one nearer me on the right was open, and as I stepped opposite to it I saw that it was a reception area or waiting room, and that it was empty. The door beyond it was also open, and I walked on up the hall. I was in uniform, so I didn't look like a burglar, and I didn't think anyone would be too alarmed by my sudden appearance. The second door in the hall opened into a dining room. This was also empty. One person had been dining at the table, but the cloth had not been cleared away, and a flickering candle showed half-filled wine-glasses and the ashes of cigarettes. The greater part of the room was in complete darkness.

"By this time I'd grown conscious of the fact that I was wandering about in a strange house, and that apparently I was alone in it. The silence of the place began to try my nerves, and in a sudden, unexplainable panic I started for the open street. As I turned, I saw a man sitting on a bench that the curve of the balustrade had hidden from me. His eyes were shut and he was sleeping soundly. A moment before, I'd been concerned because I could see no one, but at the sight of this man, I was much more bewildered.

"He was a very large Asian man, a giant in height. He was dressed in a khaki shirt that was belted at the waist and hung outside black trousers stuffed into high, black boots. He looked like a Chinese soldier in battle fatigues but what he could be doing in a private house in Toronto I had no idea. I advanced and touched the man on the shoulder, and he sprang to his feet and began talking rapidly and making deprecatory gestures. I know enough Mandarin to make out that the man was apologizing for having fallen asleep and I also was able to explain to him that I wanted to talk to the owner of the house.

"He nodded vigorously and said in English, 'Will your Excellency come this way? The princess is here.'

"I distinctly made out the word 'princess' and was somewhat puzzled. As we advanced, he noticed that the front door was standing open and, giving an exclamation of surprise, hastened toward it and closed it. Then he rapped twice on the door of what was apparently the drawing room. There was no reply to his knock, and he tapped again, then opened the door and stepped inside. He withdrew almost at once and stared at me, shaking his head.

"'She is upstairs,' he said. 'I will inform the princess of your Excellency's presence.'

"Before I could stop him, he'd turned and headed up the staircase, leaving me alone at the open door of the drawing room. I decided this adventure had gone on long enough. When I'd rang the bell, I'd expected the door to be answered by a resident who would give me directions. I certainly hadn't foreseen that I would disturb some self-styled Chinese princess, and I was beginning to wonder what kind of establishment this really was. Still, I thought I shouldn't leave without some apology, and, in the worst case, I could show my passport. They could hardly believe that a senior member of staff at an embassy had any designs upon the silverware.

"The room in which I stood was dimly lit, but I could see that, like the hall, it was hung with heavy oriental rugs. The corners were filled with house plants, and there was the unmistakable odor in the air of strange, dry scents that carried me back to the markets of Hong Kong. Near the front windows was a grand piano, and at the other end of the room, a heavily carved screen of some black wood, picked out with ivory. The screen was overhung with a canopy of silken draperies and formed a sort of alcove. In front of the alcove was a fur rug, and set on that was one of those low Turkish tables. It held two gold coffee cups. I had heard no movement from upstairs, and it must have been fully three minutes that I stood waiting, noting these details of the room and wondering at the delay and the strange silence.

"And then, suddenly, as my eye grew more used to the half-light, I saw, projecting from behind the screen as though it were stretched along the back of a sofa, the hand of a man and the lower part of his arm. I was as startled as though I'd come across a footprint on a deserted island. Evidently, the man had been sitting there ever since I had come into the room, and he must have heard the servant knocking on the door. Why hadn't he said anything? I couldn't see any more than his hand, but I had an unpleasant feeling that he'd been peering at me through the carving in the screen, and that he was still doing so. I moved my feet noisily on the floor and said tentatively, 'Excuse me.'

"There was no reply, and the hand did not stir. Apparently, the man was ignoring me, but since all I wanted to do was apologize for my intrusion and then leave, I walked up to the alcove and peered inside it. Inside the screen was a sofa piled with cushions, and the man was sitting on it. He was a young man with light yellow hair and a deeply bronzed face. He was seated with his arm stretched out along the back of the sofa, and with his head resting on a cushion. His attitude was one of complete ease. But his mouth had fallen open, and his eyes were set with an expression of utter horror. It was obvious that he was dead.

"For an instant, I was too startled to act, but I knew immediately that the man had not met his death by accident. The expression on his face was too terrible to be misinterpreted. It spoke as eloquently as words. It told me that before the end had come, he'd watched his death approach.

"I was so sure he'd been murdered that I instinctively looked for the weapon, and at the same moment, out of concern for my safety, glanced quickly behind me; but the silence of the house continued. I've seen many dead men. I was on the Mediterranean Station during the Gulf War; I was in Benghazi after the massacre. So a dead man doesn't repel me just because he's dead and, even though I knew there was no hope he was alive, I felt for his pulse by pulling open his shirt and placing my hand on his heart. My fingers instantly touched the opening of a wound, and when I withdrew them, they were wet with blood. He was in evening dress, and in the front of his shirt I found a slit, so narrow that in the dim light it was scarcely discernible. The wound was no wider than the smallest blade of a pocket knife, but narrow as it was, the weapon had been long enough to reach his heart. I felt sorry for this stranger, and at the same time selfishly concerned for my own safety and about the embarrassing publicity sure to follow. My instinct was to leave the body where it was and hide myself in the fog, but I also felt that since a succession of accidents had made me the witness to a crime, my duty was to make myself a good witness and to assist in establishing the facts of the murder.

"That it might possibly be a suicide and not a murder didn't occur to me at first. The expression on the boy's face and the fact that the weapon had disappeared were enough to convince me that he'd had no hand in his own death. I thought it important to discover who was in the house now, and who'd been in the house before I entered it. I'd seen one man leave, but all I could tell of him was that he was a young man, that he was in evening dress, and that he'd fled in such haste that he hadn't closed the door behind him.

"The Chinese soldier had been apparently asleep, and unless he'd been acting a part with supreme skill, he was innocent. There was still the supposed princess he'd expected to find, or had pretended to expect to find, in the same room as the murdered man. She must now be either upstairs with the soldier, unless she had, without his knowledge, already fled the house. When I recalled his apparently genuine surprise at not finding her in the drawing room, the latter seemed more probable. Nevertheless, I decided to search, and after a second hurried look for the weapon, I cautiously crossed the hall and went back into the dining room.

"The single candle was still flickering, and showed only the white cloth. The rest of the room was draped in shadows. I picked up the candle and, lifting it high above my head, moved around the table. My nerves were apparently so stretched that no shock could strain them further, for what I saw did not shock me. Immediately at my feet was the body of a beautiful woman, her arms flung out on either side of her. Around her throat was a great chain of diamonds, and the light played upon them and made them flash and blaze in tiny flames. But the woman who wore them was dead, and I was so sure how she had died that I dropped on my knees beside her and placed my hand on her heart. My fingers again touched the thin slit of a wound. I had no doubt in my mind that this was the 'princess.' Her features were Eurasian, her eyes black, her hair blue-black and wonderfully heavy, and her skin, even in death, was rich in color. She was an incredibly beautiful woman.

"I wanted to search again for the dagger that had been used to kill both victims, but before I could do so, I heard footsteps on the stairs, and the Chinese officer appeared in the doorway. His face wore an expression of dull bewilderment.

"'She is not there,' he said. 'The princess has gone. They have all gone.'

"'Who has gone?' I demanded. 'Who else has been here?'

"'The two Canadians.'

"'What two Canadians?' I asked. 'Who were they?'

"The man protested that he didn't know the names of the visitors, and that until this evening he'd never seen them. I tried to speak less forcefully. 'How long were they here?' I asked. 'And when did they go?'

"He pointed behind him toward the drawing room.

"'One sat there with the princess,' he said, 'and the other came after I had put the coffee in the drawing room. The men talked to each other, and the princess returned here to the table. I brought her cognac and cigarettes. Then I sat outside on the bench. It was Mao's birthday and I had been drinking. Pardon, Excellency, but I fell asleep. When I woke, your Excellency was standing by me, but the princess and the two Canadians were gone. That is all I know.'

"I believed the man was telling me the truth. His fright had passed, and he was now apparently puzzled, but not alarmed.

"'You must remember the names of the men,' I urged. 'Try to think.'

"At this he brightened and told me that both men had the same name, but he could not remember names in English. I went back and searched through the dead man's pockets. I quickly found a passport in the name of Robert Chetney."

. . .

In the St. Clair, the men at the table fell back as though a trapdoor had fallen open at their feet.

"Robert Chetney!" they exclaimed in chorus. They glanced at each other and back at the American with expressions of concern and disbelief.

"It's impossible!" cried the man in the pink shirt. "Chetney arrived back from South Africa only this week. It was reported in the papers."

The jaw of the American set in a resolute square and he pressed lips together. "You're right," he said, "Robert Chetney did arrive in Toronto this week — and yesterday evening I found his dead body. From his strong resemblance to the corpse, I concluded that the man who had run past me was Arthur, his younger brother."

Continuing his story, the American said, "For a moment, I'd forgotten the Chinese soldier, until I heard a cry behind me. I turned and saw the man gazing down at the body in abject horror.

"Before I could get up, he raced toward the front door to the street. I went after him, shouting to him to halt, but before I could reach the hall he was out into the yellow fog. I ran down the garden walk, just as the gate in front of me clicked shut. Following the sound of the man's footsteps, I raced after him across the open street. He could hear me, and he instantly stopped running. There was absolute silence. He was so near that I thought I could hear him panting, and I held my own breath to listen. But I could only make out the music I'd heard when I first lost myself.

"All I could see was the square of light from the door I'd left open behind me. As I watched it, the door slowly began to swing closed. I knew if it shut I wouldn't be able to get back in, and I rushed madly toward it, but I tripped on the curb and fell onto the sidewalk. When I rose to my feet, I was dizzy and half stunned, and though I thought then that I was moving toward the door, I know now that I probably turned directly from it; for, as I groped about, calling frantically for the police, my fingers touched nothing but the fog, and the iron railings seemed to have melted away. For a while I wandered, cursing aloud at my stupidity and crying for help. At last, a voice answered me from the fog and I found myself held in the circle of a policeman's flashlight.

"And that is the end of my adventure. What I have to tell you now is what I learned from the police."

"At the station house, I related what you've just heard. I told them that the house was set back with others from the street within a radius of two hundred yards from where I'd been found, that within fifty yards of it someone was giving a party with loud music, and that the railings in front of it were about as high as a man's waist and filed to a point. With that to work on, officers set out into the fog to search for the house, and others were dispatched to the home of Edam Chetney,

Arthur's father, to bring in Arthur for questioning. They kindly drove me back to my hotel, but I was told that I wouldn't be able to leave for Washington just yet.

"This morning, an Inspector Lyle called on me, and from him I learned the police's theory of the crime. Apparently, I'd wandered farther than I thought in the fog, for as of noon today, the house had not been found, nor had they been able to arrest Arthur. He didn't return to his father's house last night and there's no trace of him; but the theory is that the murders were committed by Arthur.

"Apparently, two years ago, Princess Jasmine, as she calls herself, and Robert Chetney were constantly together, and Chetney told his friends that they were getting married. However, when Edam Chetney heard of his son's infatuation he used his police connections to check her out.

"As a result, the police know a great deal about her and her relationship with the Chetneys. Apparently, this Princess Jasmine had once been an agent for the Chinese Third Section, but these days she was living by her wits, mostly via blackmail. Edam Chetney had shared this with his son, but either he knew it already or the woman had persuaded him not to believe it, and father and son parted after a blazing fight. Edam threatened to alter his will, leaving his entire fortune to his younger son, Arthur, if Robert saw the woman again.

"That was about eighteen months ago. Apparently, Chetney suddenly saw reason, left the princess, and went off to play bridge and travel in Africa. No word came from him, except for rumors that he had contracted Ebola. Finally, a journalist contacted the family, claiming to have seen Robert's body. Thinking Robert dead, young Arthur was recognized by the family as heir to the Chetney millions.

"On the strength of his expectations, Arthur at once began to take out enormous loans and make speculative investments. This is important: the police believe it was debt that drove Arthur to the murder of his brother. This week, as you know, Robert Chetney suddenly returned from the grave. The fact that he had been thought dead lent such importance to his return that it gave rise to those stories about him all over the Internet. Obviously, during his absence Robert had not tired of Princess Jasmine, for we know that a few hours after he arrived in Toronto, he sought her out. His brother probably figured out where he would go and followed him there, arriving while the two were having tea in the drawing room. The princess, as I learned from the servant, withdrew to the dining room, leaving the brothers alone together. What happened then one can only guess.

"Arthur knew that when it was discovered he was no longer the heir, his money troubles would overwhelm him. The police conclude that he sought out his brother to beg for money to cover his debts, but that Robert refused him. No one knew Arthur had gone to see Robert, so it is possible that, seizing his opportunity, young Arthur decided to take action to ensure himself the heir beyond further question. Crossing the hall with the same weapon, he then eliminated the sole witness to the murder. And yet," concluded the naval attaché, leaning forward and marking each word with his finger, "Arthur blundered fatally. In his haste, he left the door of the house open, giving access to the first passerby, and he forgot that the Chinese servant could identify him. In the meantime, he's disappeared completely. Somewhere in this city, in a locked and empty house, lie the body of his brother and the woman his brother loved, with their murder unavenged."

. . .

The gentleman with the pink shirt took no part in the discussion that followed the American's story. Instead, he rose and, beckoning a waiter to a far corner of the room, whispered earnestly to him until a sudden movement on the part of Professor Silver caused him to return hurriedly to the table.

"There are several points in Mr. Sears' story I want explained," said the pink shirted gentleman. "Be seated, Professor," he begged. "Let us have the opinion of an expert. I don't care what the police think, I want to know what you think."

But Professor Silver rose reluctantly from his chair.

"I should like nothing better than to discuss this," he said. "But it is most important that I proceed to the hotel. I should have been there a while ago." He turned toward the waiter and directed him to call a taxi.

The gentleman with the pink shirt looked appealingly at the American. "There are surely many details that you have not told us," he urged. "Some you have forgotten?"

Professor Silver interrupted quickly. "I trust not," he said. "I can't stop to hear them."

"The story is finished," declared the American. "Until Arthur is arrested or the bodies are found there's nothing more to tell of Chetney or Princess Jasmine."

"Of Chetney, perhaps not," interrupted the gentleman in the smoking jacket and black tie, "but there'll always be something to tell of Princess Jasmine. I know enough stories about her to fill a book. She was a most remarkable woman." He dropped the end of his cigar into his coffee cup and, taking his case from his pocket, selected a fresh cigar. As he did so, he laughed and held up the case for the others to see. It was an ordinary cigar case of well-worn pigskin, with a clasp.

"The only time I ever met her," he said, "she tried to rob me of this."

Professor Silver regarded him closely. "She tried to rob you?" he repeated.

"Of this," repeated the gentleman in the black tie. "It contained at the time a version of the Biritch document." His tone was one of mingled admiration and injury.

"The Biritch document!" exclaimed Professor Silver. He glanced quickly and suspiciously at the speaker and then at the others, but their faces gave evidence of no other emotion than that of ordinary interest.

"Yes, the very same," repeated the man with the black tie. "The original, as you may know, never leaves the possession of the academic who owns it. The Canadian government had obtained a copy by means that I cannot disclose. I was told to take it to the Chinese ambassador in Ottawa, who was to deliver it to Beijing. I am a Queen's Messenger."

"Oh! I see!" exclaimed Professor Silver in a tone of relief. "And you say this same Princess Jasmine, one of the victims of this double murder, attempted to rob you of that cigar case?"

"In which was hidden the precious document," answered the Queen's Messenger imperturbably. "It's an amusing story, and it gives you an idea of the woman's character. The robbery took place between Toronto and Ottawa."

Professor Silver interrupted him with an abrupt movement. "No, no!" he cried, shaking his arms in protest. "Don't tempt me! I really cannot listen. I must be at the Royal York in ten minutes."

"I'm sorry," said the Queen's Messenger. He turned to those seated around him. "I wonder if the other gentlemen...?" he inquired tentatively. There was a chorus of polite murmurs, and bowing his head in acknowledgment, he took a preparatory sip from his glass. At the same moment, the waiter to whom the man with the pink shirt had spoken slipped a piece of paper into his hand. He glanced at it, frowned, and threw it under the table.

The waiter looked at Professor Silver. "Your taxi is waiting, Professor," he said.

"The document was priceless to bridge historians, as it contained some interesting variations from the known version," began the Queen's Messenger. "It was a gift from the Prime Minister to celebrate—"

Professor Silver gave an exclamation of annoyance. "You're provoking me!" he said. "I really shouldn't stay ... but I must hear this." He turned to the waiter. "Tell the taxi to wait," he commanded, slipping guiltily back into his chair.

The gentleman in the pink shirt smiled blandly and rapped upon the table. "Order, gentlemen," he said. "Order for the story of the Queen's Messenger and the Biritch document."

"The document was a gift from the Prime Minister of Canada to Deng Xiaoping, who was a keen bridge player," began the Queen's Messenger. "It was to mark the anniversary of the return of Hong Kong to China in 1997. The Chinese minister of finance was going to the economic summit in Ottawa, and I was directed to travel there and hand over the document to him. But when I reached Ottawa, I found he was actually taking a brief vacation at a resort north of Toronto. His people asked me to leave the document with them at the embassy, but I had been charged to deliver it to the minister himself, so I started at once for Toronto.

"Now, how Princess Jasmine came to find out about the document, I don't know, but I can guess. As you've heard, she was once a spy in the service of the Chinese government, and after they dismissed her, she kept up her acquaintance with key members of the Chinese community in Toronto. It was probably through one of them that she learned that the document was to be sent to China, and which of the Queen's Messengers had been detailed to deliver it. She also knew something that I thought was a secret between one other person and me. The other man was also a Queen's Messenger, and a friend of mine. Until then, I'd always concealed my dispatches in a unique manner. I got the idea from a story in which a man wanted to hide a certain compromising document. He knew someone would be searching for it, so he put it in a torn envelope and stuck it on his mantelpiece, in plain view. The conclusion is that the woman who ransacked the house to find it looked everywhere but passed over the scrap of paper right under her nose.

"Sometimes the papers and packages given to us to carry about are of very great value, and sometimes they are routine government documents. As a rule, we have no knowledge of what a package contains; so, to be on the safe side, we naturally take as great a care as we would with the Crown jewels. Typically, my *confreres* carry the official packages in a briefcase, and everyone knows they are carrying something of value. Well, after hearing that story, I determined to put the government valuables in the most unlikely place that anyone would look for them. So I started to hide some of the documents they gave me among my hotel bills, and I put smaller items in an old cigar case. I bought a new case, exactly like it, for my cigars. To avoid mistakes, I had my initials engraved on both sides of the new one so the moment I touched the case, even in the dark, I could tell which one it was.

"No one knew about this except the aforementioned friend. We once left Paris together on the Orient Express: I was going to Istanbul, and he was to get off in Vienna. On the journey, I told him about my method and showed him my cigar case. After the robbery, I asked him about the secret I had shared with him. He was greatly distressed and admitted that he had shared the idea with Princess Jasmine. He had had no idea she was a spy, as she seemed just a very attractive woman he was trying to impress. That's how I determined who it was who had robbed me, and how she could have known that the document was concealed in my cigar case.

"I avoid air travel whenever possible, so I took the train for Toronto that left Ottawa at ten in the morning. When I travel at night, I generally tell the conductor that I am a Queen's Messenger, and get a sleeper to myself. But in the daytime, I'm not so concerned. That morning I had found an empty compartment, and I had tipped the steward to keep everyone else out, not from any fear of losing the document, but because I wanted to smoke surreptitiously. I began to arrange my things and make myself comfortable. The document in the cigar case was in the inside pocket of my jacket, and as that made a bulky package I took it out, intending to put it in my dispatch bag. It's a small satchel, like those handbags that couriers carry. I wear it slung from a strap across my shoulder, and, no matter whether I am sitting or walking, it never leaves me.

"I took the cigar case that held the document from my inside pocket, and the case that held the cigars out of the satchel, and while I was searching through it for a box of matches, I laid the two cases beside me on the seat. At that moment the train started, but at the same instant there was a rattle at the door of the compartment, and a couple of porters lifted and shoved a woman through the door and hurled her luggage in after her.

"Instinctively, I reached for the case with the document. I shoved it quickly into the satchel and snapped the spring lock. Then I put the cigars in the pocket of my coat, thinking that now I'd probably not be allowed to enjoy them. The newcomer's purse had fallen at my feet and a tube of lipstick had landed at my side. I thought if I hid the fact that the lady was not welcome, and at once started to be civil, she might permit me to smoke. So I picked her purse off the floor and asked her where I should put it. As I spoke I looked at her for the first time and saw that she was a remarkably attractive Asian lady.

"She smiled charmingly, then arranged her own things about her and, opening her purse, took out a gold cigarette case.

"'Do you object to my smoking?' she asked.

"I laughed and assured her I'd been hoping she would allow me to smoke.

"'Would you try one of these?' she asked. 'They're custom-made for my husband in Russia, and they're supposed to be very good.'

"I thanked her and took one from her case, and I found it so much better than my own that I continued to smoke her cigarettes throughout the rest of the journey. I must say that we got on very well. I judged from the fact of her traveling first class, and from her manner, that she was someone of importance. At first she read a novel, and then she made comment on the scenery, and finally we began to discuss places we had traveled. She talked of the great cities of Europe and seemed to know them all well. She volunteered nothing about herself except that she frequently made use of expressions like, 'When my husband was stationed at Vienna,' or, 'When my husband was promoted to Rome.' Then she said to me, 'I have seen you at Monte Carlo. I was there when you almost won the World Bridge Championship.' I told her that I was not an expert bridge player, and she gave a little start of surprise. 'Oh! I beg your pardon,' she said, 'I thought you were Eric Murray, the Canadian champion.' As a matter of fact, I do look something like Murray, but I know now that her purpose was to make me think that she had no idea who I really was. She needn't have worried, for I certainly was not suspicious of her, and was only too pleased to have so charming a companion.

"'I see you're reading Zia's book,' she continued. 'A few years ago, I was kibitzing Zia during the final round of the Spingold, when I watched him play a hand, here, I will write it down for you.

Dealer East. Both vul.

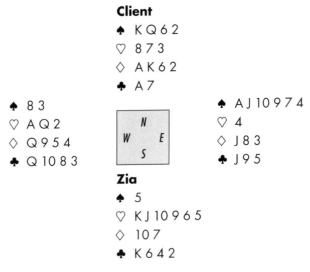

	Client
	♠ K Q 6 2
	♡ 8 7 3
	◇ A K 6 2
	♣ A 7

West		East
♠ 8 3		♠ A J 10 9 7 4
♡ A Q 2		♡ 4
◇ Q 9 5 4		◇ J 8 3
♣ Q 10 8 3		♣ J 9 5

	Zia
	♠ 5
	♡ K J 10 9 6 5
	◇ 10 7
	♣ K 6 4 2

West	North	East	South
		2♠	pass
pass	2NT	pass	4♡
all pass			

"Zia jumped to 4♡ because he didn't want North to be declarer on the deal. The opening lead was the ♠8 and as soon as the dummy went down, Zia called for the ♠K from dummy. East won his ace and switched unerringly to his small trump. Zia put in the ♡9, losing to the ♡Q, and West continued with ace and another heart. Declarer won the third round of hearts in dummy, discarded a club on the ♠Q and ruffed a spade. These cards remained:

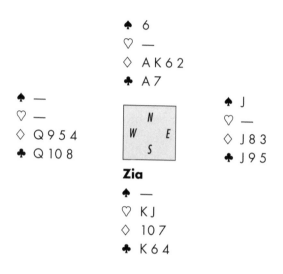

♠ 6
♡ —
◇ A K 6 2
♣ A 7

♠ —
♡ —
◇ Q 9 5 4
♣ Q 10 8

♠ J
♡ —
◇ J 8 3
♣ J 9 5

Zia

♠ —
♡ K J
◇ 10 7
♣ K 6 4

"'It would appear that there is an inescapable club loser and 4♡ must go down one,' I said.

"'Not with Zia at the helm.' She smiled. 'Zia played East for his most likely original shape of 6=1=3=3 and West for a corresponding 2=3=4=4 distribution. When the ♡J is played, West is in trouble. If he discards a diamond, dummy discards the ♠6 and declarer plays the ◇AK and ruffs a diamond to establish the ◇6 as the tenth trick. So West discards a club, and dummy the ◇2. Next comes the ♡K, and West's discard is irrelevant now but dummy throws a diamond. Now playing the ◇AK squeezes East in the blacks. Zia played West to hold at least four diamonds, for otherwise there is no squeeze.'

"Having discovered our mutual interest in bridge, the journey continued pleasantly enough. The one thing that should have made me suspicious was the fact that at every station she made some trivial excuse to get me out of the compartment. She wanted water, or a snack, or something else each time, and would I be so very kind as to go and bring her whatever it was she pretended she wanted?

"I had taken my suitcase from the rack to get out my book, and had left it on the seat opposite to mine and furthest from her. Once, when I came back from buying her a cup of chocolate or from some other fool errand, I found her standing at my end of the compartment with both hands on the suitcase. She looked at me without so much as winking an eye, and shoved the case carefully into a corner. 'Your bag slipped off onto the floor,' she said. 'If you've got any bottles in it, you had better look and see that they're not broken.'

"And I give you my word, I was such an ass that I did open the case and look all through it. She must have thought I was a total idiot. But in spite of everything, she couldn't gain anything by sending me away, because what she wanted was in the dispatch case, and every time she sent me away, the dispatch case went with me.

"After the incident of the suitcase, her manner began to change. Either she had had time to look through it in my absence or she had seen everything it held when I was examining it for breakages. From that moment, she must have been certain that the cigar case was in the bag that never left my body, and from that time on she was probably plotting how to get it from me.

"Her anxiety became apparent. She ceased talking and answered me irritably or at random when I spoke. No doubt her mind was entirely occupied with her plan. The end of our journey was drawing rapidly nearer, and her time for action was being cut down with the speed of the express train. Even I, unsuspicious as I was, noticed that something was very wrong with her. I really believe that before we reached Toronto, if I had not given her the chance she wanted, she might have stuck a knife in me and rolled me out on the rails. But I thought the long journey had tired her. I suggested that it was a very tedious trip and offered her some of my cognac.

"She started to say no, and then suddenly her eyes lit up, and she exclaimed, 'Yes, thank you, if you will be so kind.'

"My flask was in the dispatch case. I placed the case on my lap and slipped back the catch with my thumb. As I keep my travel documents in the bag, I am so frequently opening it that I never bother to lock it, and the fact that it is strapped to me has always been sufficient protection. But I can appreciate now what a satisfaction it must have been to that woman when she saw that the bag opened without a key.

"Early in the journey, I had felt chilly and had been wearing a light sweater. But now the compartment became hot and stuffy, so I stood up and, after first slipping the strap of the bag over my head, placed the bag on the seat next to me and pulled off the sweater. I don't blame myself for being careless; the bag was still within reach of my hand, and nothing would have happened if at that exact moment the train had not made another stop. It was the combination of my removing the bag and our entering the station at the same instant that gave Princess Jasmine the chance she wanted to rob me, and of course she was clever enough to take it. The train ran into the station at a fair speed and came to a sudden stop. I had just thrown my sweater onto the rack and had reached out my hand for the bag. In an instant I would have had the strap around my shoulder. But at that moment, the princess threw down the window and beckoned wildly at the people on the platform.

"'Margaret!' she called, 'Margaret! Here I am. Come here! This way!' She turned to me in excitement and continued pointing outside and beckoning me with her hand. 'My friend!' she cried. 'She is looking for me. She looked in the window without seeing me. Go, please, and bring her back.' There certainly was something about that woman's tone that made one jump to attention. When she was giving orders, you had no chance to think of anything else. So I rushed out on my errand of mercy and then rushed back again to ask what the woman looked like.

"'Black,' she answered, rising and blocking the door of the compartment. 'All in black, with a woolen hat!' The train waited three minutes at Guildford, and in that time I suppose I must have rushed up to over twenty women and asked, 'Are you Margaret?' The only reason I wasn't handed over to the police must have been that they probably thought I was crazy.

"When I jumped back into the compartment the princess was seated where I had left her, but her eyes were burning with happiness. She placed her hand on my arm almost affectionately and said, 'You are very kind. I am so sorry to have troubled you.'

"I protested that every woman on the platform was dressed in black. 'Indeed, I am so sorry,' she said, laughing, and she continued to laugh until she began to breathe so quickly that I thought she was going to faint.

"I can see now that the last part of that journey must have been a terrible half-hour for her. She had the cigar case, but she knew that if I were to open my bag, even at the last minute, and miss the case, I would know that she had taken it. I had placed the document in the bag at the very moment she had entered the compartment, and no one else had been in it since. So when we reached Toronto, she would be $25,000 richer or she would be arrested. I don't envy her state of mind during those last few minutes. It must have been hell.

"I saw that something was off, and in my innocence I even wondered if she had drunk a little too much of my cognac. For she suddenly developed into a brilliant conversationalist, and applauded and laughed at everything I said, firing off questions at me like a machine gun, so that I had no time to think of anything else. I wondered how I could have considered her an agreeable traveling companion. I would have preferred to be locked in with a lunatic. I don't like to think how she would have acted if I had made a move to examine the bag, but as I had it safely strapped around me again, I did not open it, and I reached Toronto alive. As we drew into the station, she shook hands with me and grinned at me like a Cheshire cat.

"'I cannot tell you,' she said, 'how much I have to thank you for.'

"What do you think of that for impudence?

"I offered to put her in a taxi, but she said she must contact Margaret first, and that she hoped we should meet again at the hotel. So I headed off by myself, wondering who she was and whether Margaret was her keeper. The train up to Muskoka was not until the next morning, and as I wanted to stroll around downtown, I thought I'd better put the document in the safe at the hotel. As soon as I reached my room, I locked the door, placed the dispatch case on the table, and opened it. I felt among the things at the top of it but failed to find the cigar case. I shoved my hand in deeper and stirred the things about, but still I did not find it. A cold wave swept down my spine, and a sort of emptiness came to the pit of my stomach. I said to myself, 'Don't be an idiot! Pull yourself together, pull yourself together. Take the things out, one at a time. It's there, of course it's there.'

"So I began very carefully to pick out the things one by one, but after five seconds I couldn't stand it another instant, and I threw everything onto the bed. I pulled the things about and shuffled and rearranged them, but it was no use. The cigar case was gone. I knew that I had put it in the bag. I sat down and tried to think. I remembered I'd put it in just as that woman had entered the compartment, and I had been alone with her ever since, so it was she who had robbed me. But how? It had never left my shoulder. Then I remembered that I had taken it off to remove my sweater and hadn't had it for the few moments that I was searching for Margaret. I gave a roar like a mad bull and I jumped down the stairs six steps at a time.

"I demanded of the person at the front desk to tell me if a lady traveler, possibly Chinese, had just checked in. As I expected, she hadn't. I sprang into a cab and inquired at two other hotels, and then I saw the folly of trying to catch her without outside help, and I went to the police. I told my story, and the cretin in charge asked me to calm myself and wanted to take notes. I told him this was no time for taking notes, this required immediate action! He became angry at that, and I demanded to be taken at once to his chief. The chief, he said, was very busy and could not see me. So I showed him my government ID. In eleven years, I had used it only once before. I stated in pretty forceful language that I was a Queen's Messenger, and that if the chief of police did not see me instantly, he would lose his official head. The fellow jumped off his high horse at that and took me to his chief — who turned out to be a very intelligent man.

"I explained that I had been robbed of a document that the Prime Minister was sending as a gift to the People's Republic of China. I pointed out to him that if he succeeded in capturing the thief, he would be made for life. He wasn't the sort to let a good opportunity pass by. With visions of Canadian and Chinese decorations adorning his chest, he began yelling orders like the captain of a steamer in a fog. He sent the princess's description to all the city police stations and ordered a search of every train and bus leaving Toronto. He had the car rental agencies checked. He ordered that all passengers on outgoing flights be examined, and requested that the managers of every hotel and motel send in a complete guest list within the hour. While I was standing there he must have given at least a hundred orders and sent out enough policemen to have captured an army. Once they had been dispatched, he assured me that my princess was as good as arrested.

"The chief told me to return to my hotel and await his call — she would be found within an hour, he assured me. I thanked him and left. But I didn't share his confidence. I knew that she was a very clever woman and a match for any of us. It was all very well for him to be jubilant: he had not lost the Biritch document and had everything to gain if he found it. I, even if he did recover the document, would be only where I was before I lost it, and if he did not recover it, I was ruined. I had always prided myself on my record. In eleven years, I had never mislaid an envelope or missed a delivery deadline. And it wasn't a thing that could be hushed up, either. It was too conspicuous, too spectacular. It was sure to be all over the Internet. I saw myself ridiculed, perhaps dismissed, even suspected of having taken the thing myself.

"I was walking past a downtown pub, and I felt so sick and miserable that I sat down at a sidewalk table to order a pick-me-up. I considered that if I took one drink I would probably, in my present state of mind, not want to stop until I reached twenty, and decided I'd better not. But my nerves were jumping like a frightened rabbit, and I felt I needed something to quiet them or I would go crazy. I reached for my cigarette case, which suddenly seemed hardly adequate, so I put it back again and took out my cigar case, in which I keep only the strongest and blackest cigars. Upon opening it, my fingers made contact with a thin envelope. I rose slowly from my chair. My heart stood perfectly still. I didn't dare to look, but slid my fingers further inside and felt a layer of cotton, followed by the heavy paper of the Biritch document!

"I cried out, as though I had been hit in the face, and fell back into my chair. I spread out the document on the table; I could not believe it was real. I believe I almost kissed it. I made so much noise that people crowded around me to see what was happening. The manager came over to deal with the disturbance, but I was so happy I didn't care. I laughed, gave him a handful of bills, and told him to buy everyone a drink. Then I rushed off to the police station to see the chief. I felt badly for him. He'd been so happy at the opportunity to prove himself, and he would be disappointed when he learned I'd sent him on a wild goose chase.

"But now that I had the document, I didn't want the police to find the woman. I was actually hoping she would get clear away, because if she were caught, the truth would come out. I was likely to get a sharp reprimand, and certainly I would be laughed at. I could see now how it had happened. In my haste to hide the document when the woman arrived in the compartment, I had shoved the cigars into the dispatch case and the document into the pocket of my coat. Now that I had it safe again, it seemed a very natural mistake. I doubted, however, that my superiors would think so. I was afraid they might not appreciate the beautiful simplicity of my secret hiding place. So, when I reached the police station and found the princess to be still at large, I was more than relieved.

"As I expected, the chief was extremely chagrined when he learned that there was nothing for him to do. I was feeling so happy and hated to think anyone else miserable, so I suggested that this attempt to steal the document might be only the first in a series of such attempts, and that I would not be safe until my mission was completed. I still needed his help.

"I winked at the chief and the chief smiled back at me, and together we went north to Deerhurst in a police car surrounded by a guard of twelve detectives and twelve uniformed officers, the chief and I drinking champagne all the way. We marched together up to the resort where the Chinese minister was relaxing, closely surrounded by our escort of Toronto's finest, and delivered the document with the most profound ceremony. The minister was immensely impressed, and when we hinted that I already had been made the object of an attack by thieves, he assured us that the People's Republic would not prove ungrateful. I wrote a personal letter praising the invaluable services of the chief to the minister of foreign affairs, and they gave him Canadian and Chinese merits enough to satisfy even a governor general. So, though he never caught the woman, he received his reward."

. . .

The Queen's Messenger paused and surveyed the faces of those about him in some embarrassment.

"But the crux of it is," he added, "that the story must have got out, because while the princess obtained nothing from me but a cigar case and five excellent cigars, a few weeks later, the Chinese embassy sent me a gold cigar case with my initials on it. Made in China, of course, yet still quite expensive looking. And I don't yet know whether that was a coincidence or whether the minister wanted me to know that he knew I'd been carrying the document around in my cigar case. What do you fellows think?"

Professor Silver rose, disapproval written in every lineament of his face. "I thought your story would concern the murder," he said. "Had I imagined it would have nothing whatsoever to do with it, I would not have remained." He pushed back his chair and bowed stiffly. "I wish you a good evening," he said.

There was a chorus of remonstrance, and under cover of the answering protests, a waiter slipped another piece of paper into the hand of the gentleman with the pink shirt, who scanned the lines written on it and tore it into tiny fragments.

The American raised his hand and asked, "What is the Biritch document and why is this copy worth $25,000?"

"It's a myth," replied the man in the pink shirt, "an old bridge player's tale. It has the same pedigree as an email from Nigeria asking for help in retrieving an inheritance."

"Not so!" Professor Silver interjected, turning back. "I have seen it myself."

"But what makes it worth $25,000?" persisted the American.

"The Biritch document is the earliest published description of the rules of bridge, and if this particular version contained some differences from the established rules, it might throw real light on the origin of the game — something that, as you know, is a matter of dispute. To a collector, it might well be worth well in excess of the sum named," replied the professor.

The youngest member, who had remained an interested but silent observer during the tale of the Queen's Messenger, raised his hand commandingly.

"Professor," he cried, "in justice to Arthur Chetney, I must ask to be heard. He's been accused in our hearing of a serious crime and I insist that you remain until you've heard me clear his name."

"You can clear his name?" cried Professor Silver.

"Yes," answered the young man briskly. "I would have spoken sooner," he explained, "but that I thought this gentleman" — he inclined his head toward the Queen's Messenger — "was about to contribute some facts of which I was ignorant. But he's told us nothing, and so I take up the tale at the point where Commander Sears laid it down. It may seem strange to you that I'm able to add the sequel to his story. I'm the junior partner in the law firm of Jarndyce and Jarndyce. We have looked after legal matters for the Chetneys for the last fifty years. Nothing, no matter how unimportant, that concerns Edam Chetney and his two sons, is unknown to us, and naturally I'm acquainted with every detail of the terrible catastrophe of last night."

. . .

Professor Silver, bewildered but eager, sank back into his chair. "Will it take long?" he demanded.

"I'll try to be brief," said the young lawyer. "And," he added, in a tone that gave his words almost the weight of a threat, "I promise to be interesting."

"There's no need to promise that," said Professor Silver. "I find it much too interesting as it is." He glanced ruefully at the clock and turned his eyes quickly from it. "Tell the driver of that taxi," he called to the waiter, "to turn on his meter and leave it running."

Young Mr. Jarndyce began: "As you have probably heard, Edam Chetney has been seriously ill — indeed, at the point of death for the last three days. Every hour he seems to grow weaker, although his mind has remained clear and active. Late yesterday evening, his assistant called my father to ask him to come at once and to bring with him certain papers. What these papers concern is not important; I mention them only to explain how it was that last night I happened to be at Edam Chetney's bedside. I accompanied my father to Chetney House, but when we arrived, Mr. Chetney was sleeping, and his doctor refused to wake him. So we all gathered in the library to wait until he awoke.

"At about one o'clock in the morning, Inspector Lyle arrived to question Arthur regarding the murder of his brother. You can imagine our shock. Like everyone else, I had learned this week that Robert

Chetney was not dead, but that he had returned to Canada. And I had been told that Arthur had gone to the Royal York to look for his brother and tell him to come to see his father at once. But Arthur hadn't returned. None of us knew where Princess Jasmine had lived, so we couldn't help with the discovery of Robert Chetney's body. We spent a most miserable night, hastening to the window whenever a cab came onto the street, in the hope that it was Arthur returning to explain the facts that pointed to him as the murderer. I'm a friend of Arthur's — I was with him at university and we've played bridge together often — and I refused to believe for an instant that he was capable of such a crime; but as a lawyer I could see that the evidence was strongly against him.

"Toward early morning, Edam Chetney awoke and was feeling so much better he declared himself to be no nearer death than we were. Normally, this would have relieved us greatly, but none of us could think of anything save the death of his elder son and of the charge that hung over Arthur.

"As long as Inspector Lyle remained in the house, my father decided that I, as one of the legal advisers of the family, should also stay. But there was little for either of us to do. Arthur didn't return, and nothing happened until late this morning, when Lyle received word that the Chinese soldier had been arrested, and left to question him. He returned within the hour and informed me that the man had refused to talk about the events of the night before or of himself and Princess Jasmine. He would not even give them the address of her house.

"'I assured him that he was not suspected of the crime,' Lyle told me, 'but he would still tell me nothing.'

"There were no other developments until two o'clock this afternoon, when we heard that Arthur had been found. It turns out he had been in a traffic accident and subsequently admitted to St. Michael's Hospital. Lyle and I drove there together and found him propped up in bed with his head bound in a bandage. He'd been brought in the night before, unconscious, by the driver of a BMW that had run into him in the fog. Arthur had no ID on him, and it was not until he came to his senses this afternoon that anyone had been able to contact his family. Lyle at once informed him of his rights, but as his lawyer, I instructed Arthur to tell us all he knew of the occurrences of last night. It was obvious to everyone that the fact of his brother's death was of much greater concern to him than that he might be accused of his murder.

"'That—"Arthur said of the accusation contemptuously, 'that is nonsense! We parted on better terms than we've been on for years. I'll tell you all that happened — not simply to clear myself, but to help you to find out the truth.'

"His story was as follows. He had spent the previous days at his father's bedside, and it was not until last night that he learned that his brother was alive and at the bridge tournament. He drove there at once but was told that his brother had gone out at about eight o'clock, without giving any clue to his destination. Arthur decided to look for his brother at the home of the Princess Jasmine — though he had never visited it, he knew its address. He accordingly hailed a taxi and rode in that direction, as far as the fog would permit the cab to go, and walked the rest of the way, reaching the house about nine o'clock. He rang the bell, and his brother came out and welcomed him. He was followed by Princess Jasmine, who received Arthur most cordially.

"'You brothers will have much to talk about,' she said. 'I shall wait in the dining room. When you have finished, let me know.'

"As soon as she had left them, Arthur told his brother that their father was not expected to live out the night, and that he must come at once.

"'This is not the time to remember your quarrel,' Arthur said to Robert. 'You've come back from the dead just in time to make your peace with him before he dies.'

"'I didn't know Father was ill or I would've gone to him the minute I arrived,' Robert said. 'I'll follow you back as soon as I've said goodbye to Jasmine. This is the end — after this I shall never see her again.'

"'Do you mean that?' Arthur cried.

"'Yes,' Robert answered. 'When I returned to Toronto, I had no intention of seeking her out, and I am here only because she misled me.' He then told Arthur that he had broken up with the princess even before he went to South Africa, when he found out that she had been seeing someone else.

"'The whole two years I had spent trying to obtain Father's approval of our marriage, she was having an affair with a Russian diplomat.'

"'Yet here you are with her tonight,' Arthur protested.

"'I know,' his brother replied. 'I received a message from her at the tournament saying she had just learned of my arrival and begging me to come to her at once. She wrote that she was in great trouble, dying of an incurable illness, and without friends or money. She begged me, for old times' sake, to come to her assistance. So I drove here and found her, as you see, as beautiful as ever, in very good health, and, from the look of the house, in no need of money.

"'I asked her why she'd told me that she was dying in a garret, and she laughed and said she'd been afraid that I would not see her. That was where we were when you arrived. And now,' Robert added, 'I'll say goodbye to her, and you'd better go home. I'll follow you as soon as I can, but when she learns that this is the end, she may make a scene. Tell Father I'll be there ten minutes after you.'

"'That,' Arthur told me, 'is the way we parted. I was happy to see him alive again, I was happy to think he had returned in time to make up with my father, and I was happy that at last he was clear of that woman.' He turned to Inspector Lyle, who was sitting at the foot of the bed taking notes.

"'Why,' he cried, 'would I choose that moment of all others to send my brother back to the grave?' For a moment, the inspector did not answer him. I don't know if any of you gentlemen are acquainted with Inspector Lyle, but if not, I'll tell you, he's a very remarkable man. Our firm often works with him and my father has the greatest possible respect for him. He often imagines himself as the criminal, imagines how he would act under the same circumstances, and he imagines so well that he generally finds the man he wants. I've often told Lyle that if he weren't a detective, he would've been a great success as a writer or a playwright.

"Anyway, Lyle hesitated for a moment and then told Arthur exactly what the case against him was.

"'Ever since your brother was reported as having died in Africa,' he said, 'you have been borrowing money on the strength of your inheritance. Robert's arrival last night turned your IOUs into waste paper. You were suddenly in debt for much more than you could ever possibly pay. No one knew that you and your brother had met at Princess Jasmine's. But you knew that your father was not expected to live out the night, and that if your brother were dead also, you would be saved from complete ruin.'

"'Oh! That's what you think, is it?' Arthur cried. 'And for me to become solvent, was it necessary that the woman should die, too?'

"'I assume,' Lyle answered, 'that she was a witness to the murder.'

"'Then why didn't I kill the servant as well? The Chinese soldier — he was there too,' Arthur said.

"'Perhaps you knew he was asleep and saw nothing.'

"'You really believe that?' Arthur demanded.

"'It is not a question of what I believe,' Lyle said gravely. 'It is a question for a jury.'

"'Ridiculous!' Arthur cried. Before we could stop him, he sprang out of his bed and began pulling on his clothes. 'You think you can keep me here,' he shouted, 'and charge me with murder? I'm going with you to that house! When you find those bodies, I'll be beside you. It is my right. He's my brother. He's been murdered, and I can tell you who murdered him. That woman murdered him. First she ruined his life and then she killed him. For years she plotted to make herself his wife, and last night, when he told her he knew about the Russian and that she would never see him again, she stabbed him, and then, in remorse, killed herself. She murdered him, I tell you, and I promise you that we will find the knife she used near her — perhaps still in her hand. What do you say to that?'

"Lyle turned his head away and stared down at the floor. 'I might say,' he answered, 'that you placed it there.'

Arthur gave a cry of anger, then pitched forward and fell. Lyle carried him back to the bed again. He left him under guard with the doctors and we drove at once to the address he had given us. We found the house not ten minutes' walk from St. Michael's Hospital. It stands just off University Avenue, near several other hospitals.

When we reached the house, Lyle broke one of the windows on the ground floor, and we scrambled in. We found ourselves in the reception room, which was the first room on the right of the hall. The ashes of a fire were visible behind the colored glass and red silk shades, and when the daylight streamed in after us, it gave the hall a hideously dissipated look, like the lobby of a theater at a matinee. The house was oppressively silent, and because we knew why it was so silent, we spoke in whispers. When Lyle turned the handle of the drawing room door, I felt as though someone had put his hand on my throat. But I followed close at his shoulder and saw the body of Robert Chetney at the foot of the sofa, just as Commander Sears here described it. In the drawing room, we found Princess Jasmine. But neither of us, although we searched the floor on our hands and knees, could find the weapon that had killed her.

"'For Arthur's sake,' I said, 'I would give a thousand dollars if we had found the knife in her hand, as he said we would.'

"'The fact that we didn't find it there,' Lyle answered, 'is to my mind the strongest indication that he's telling the truth — that he left the house before the murder took place. He's not a fool; if had he stabbed his brother and this woman, he would have seen that by placing the knife near her he could help make it appear to be a murder-suicide. Besides, Arthur insisted that the proof of his innocence would be our finding the knife here. He would not have urged that if he knew we would not find it. But this is no suicide — we're looking at a double murder.'

"While he spoke, Lyle and I searched every corner, studying the details of each room. I was so afraid that he would make deductions prejudicial to Arthur without telling me that I never left his side. I was determined to see everything he saw, and, if possible, to prevent his interpreting it the wrong way. He finally finished his examination, and we sat down together in the drawing room. He took out his notebook and read aloud all Mr. Sears had told him of the murder, and what we had just learned from Arthur. We compared the two accounts, word for word, and weighed statement with statement. But I could not determine from anything Lyle said which of the two versions he had decided to believe.

"'We're trying to build a house of blocks,' he exclaimed, 'with half of the blocks missing. Until the Chinese soldier is ready to talk, I refuse to speculate further.'

"'He was drunk and asleep,' I objected. 'He saw nothing.'

"Lyle hesitated and then made up his mind to be frank with me.

"'I don't know that he was either drunk or asleep,' he answered. 'Commander Sears thought him stupid, but he could be just a clever actor. What was his position in this house? What was his real duty here? Suppose it was actually to watch this woman. Suppose he wasn't working for the woman but someone else entirely — let's see where that leads us. This house has a mysterious owner, who lives in Moscow, the unknown Russian of Jasmine's affair. He's the man who bought this house for her, who sent these rugs and curtains from Europe to furnish it for her after his own tastes, and, I believe, it was he who placed the soldier here, ostensibly to serve her, but in reality to keep an eye on her. Interpol doesn't know who this man is, and neither do the Russian police.'

"Lyle pointed at the modern French paintings and the heavy silk rugs that hung upon the walls.

"'He's a man of taste and obviously wealthy,' he said, 'not the sort of man to send a stupid peasant to guard the woman he loves. I don't agree with Mr. Sears' view that the guard is an idiot. I think he's the protector of his employer's honor, or, let's say, of his employer's property, whether that property is real estate or a mistress. Last night, after Arthur had gone, the servant was left alone with Robert Chetney and Princess Jasmine. From where he sat, he could hear Robert Chetney saying goodbye, because I think he understands English as well as you or I. Let's imagine that he hears her begging Robert not to leave her, reminding him that he wanted to marry her, and let's suppose that he hears Chetney tell her that he knows about this Russian admirer — the servant's employer. He hears the woman declare that this unknown Russian is nothing to her, that there's no man she loves but him. Suppose Robert believed her, suppose his former infatuation for her returned, and that in a moment of weakness he forgave her and took her in his arms. That's the moment the Russian feared and why he placed his watchdog over the princess; and when the moment comes, the watchdog does his job and kills them both. What do you think?' Lyle demanded. 'Wouldn't that explain both murders?'

"I was willing to hear any theory that pointed to anyone else but Arthur, but Lyle's explanation was utterly fantastic. I told him that it certainly showed imagination, but that he couldn't arrest a man for what he imagined he had done.

"'No,' Lyle answered, 'but I can make it clear to him that I believe he is the murderer. I think that will open his mouth. A man will usually talk to defend himself,' he said, 'I must get back and question him again. There is nothing more to do here.'

"He rose and I followed him out the door, and in another minute we would have been on our way. But just as he opened the street door, a mail carrier walked past the house on the sidewalk. Lyle stopped, with an exclamation of chagrin.

"'How stupid of me!' he exclaimed. He turned quickly and pointed to a narrow slit cut in the brass plate of the front door. 'I never thought to look at the mail that came this morning. I've been extremely careless,' he said in great excitement.

"Calling after the mailman, he quickly determined that several letters had indeed been delivered about eleven that very morning. He stepped back into the hall and pulled at the lid of the mailbox, which hung on the inside of the door.

"'Let's examine these letters. We might get lucky here and discover the name of the owner of this house.'

"The lid popped open under his hand, but the box was empty! I don't know how long we stood staring stupidly at each other, but Lyle recovered first. He seized me by the arm and pointed excitedly into the empty box.

"'Do you see what that means?' he cried. 'It means that someone has been here ahead of us. Someone entered this house after eleven o'clock this morning, not three hours before we came.'

"'It was the Chinese soldier!' I exclaimed.

"'The Chinese soldier has been under arrest all day!' Lyle cried. 'And Arthur has been in his bed at the hospital. That's his alibi. There's someone else — someone we do not suspect — and that someone is the murderer! He came back here either to obtain those letters because he knew they would convict him or to remove something he had left here at the time of the murder, something incriminating — the weapon, perhaps — or some personal article.'

"'How do we know,' I whispered, 'that he's not hidden here now?'

"'No, I'm sure he isn't!' Lyle answered. 'I've been through this house thoroughly. Still,' he added, 'we've got to go over it again. We have a real clue now, so we have to forget the others and follow only this one.' As he spoke, he began again to search the drawing room, turning over even the books on the tables and the music on the piano.

"'Whoever this man is,' he said over his shoulder, 'we know that he has a key to the front door. That shows us he either lives here or comes here when he wishes. The only other person who would have a key to the house lives in Moscow. At the time of the murder he was thousands of miles away.'

"Lyle interrupted himself suddenly with a sharp cry and turned to me with his eyes flashing.

"'But was he?' he cried. 'How do we know that last night he wasn't in Toronto, here in this very house when Jasmine and Chetney met?'

"He stood staring at me without seeing me, muttering and arguing with himself.

"'Quiet!' he cried, as I ventured to interrupt him. 'It's obvious now. It wasn't the servant but his employer, the Russian himself, and it was he who came back for the letters. He came back for them because he knew they would convict him. We must have those letters. If we find them, we shall have found the murderer.' As he spoke, he ran around the room with one hand held in front of him. He pulled old letters from the writing desk and ran them over as swiftly as a gambler deals out cards; dropped on his knees before the fireplace and dragged out the dead ashes with his bare fingers, and then, with a low, worried cry, like a hound on a scent, he ran back to the wastepaper basket and shook it out upon the floor. Instantly, he gave a shout of triumph and, separating a number of torn pieces from the others, held them up before me.

"'Look!' he cried. 'See? Here are five letters, torn across. The Russian didn't stop to read them: he left them still sealed. I've been wrong. He didn't return for the letters. He couldn't have known their value. He must have returned for some other reason, and, as he was leaving, saw the letterbox, and taking the letters, held them together — so — and tore them twice across, and then, as the fire had gone out, tossed them into this basket. Look! Here in the upper corner of this piece is a Russian stamp. This is his own letter — unopened!'

"We examined the Russian stamp and found it had been cancelled in Moscow four days ago. The envelope was made of blue paper, and we had no difficulty finding the two other parts to it. We drew the torn pieces of the letter from them and joined them together side by side. There were but two lines of writing, and this was the message: 'I am flying on Air Canada, and I shall see you at your home after dinner Monday.'

"'That was last night!' Lyle cried. 'He arrived twelve hours ahead of his letter — but it came in time to convict him!'

...

The man in the pink shirt struck the table with his hand.

"The name!" he demanded. "How was it signed? What was the man's name?"

The young solicitor rose to his feet and, leaning forward, stretched out his arm.

"There was no name," he cried. "The letter was signed with only two initials. But engraved at the top of the sheet was the man's address. That address was the U.S. Embassy, Office of the Naval Attaché, and the initials," he shouted, his voice rising into an exultant and bitter cry, "were those of the gentleman who sits opposite, who told us that he was the first to find the murdered bodies, Commander Ripley Sears!"

A strained and awful hush followed the solicitor's words, which seemed to vibrate in the air like a twanging bowstring that had just hurled its arrow. Professor Silver, pale and staring, drew away with an exclamation. His eyes were fixed on the American with fascinated horror. But the American emitted a sigh of great content and sank comfortably into the arms of his chair. He clapped his hands softly together.

"Very nice!" he murmured. "I never guessed where you were heading. You fooled me, you certainly fooled me!"

The man with the pink shirt leaned forward with a nervous gesture.

"Hush! Be careful!" he whispered. But at that instant, for the third time, a waiter hastening through the room handed him a piece of paper, which he scanned eagerly. The message on the paper read, "The final quarter has begun."

The man with the pink shirt gave a mighty shout and tossed the paper from him onto the table. "Hooray!" he cried. "The last few boards are under way, and the professor is still here! We are going to win!"

He caught up his glass and slapped the American violently on the shoulder. He nodded joyously at him, at the lawyer, and at the Queen's

Messenger. "Gentlemen, to you!" he cried. "My thanks and my congratulations!" He drank deep from the glass and breathed forth a long sigh of satisfaction and relief.

"Wait!" protested the Queen's Messenger, shaking his finger violently at the lawyer, "that story doesn't work. You talked so fast I couldn't make out what it was all about. And I'll bet you that evidence wouldn't hold up in court. Your story is nonsense. Now, my story might have happened; my story bore the mark…"

In the joy of creation, the storytellers had forgotten their audience, until a sudden exclamation from Professor Silver caused them to turn guiltily toward him. His face was knit with lines of anger, doubt, and amazement.

"What does this mean?" he cried. "Is this a joke? If you know this man is a murderer, why is he at large? Is this a game you have been playing? Explain yourselves at once."

The American, with first a glance at the others, rose and bowed courteously.

"I am not a murderer, Professor, believe me," he said. "You need not be alarmed. As a matter of fact, at this moment I am much more afraid of you than you could possibly be of me. I apologize. I assure you we meant no disrespect. We have been matching stories, that is all, pretending that we are people we are not, endeavoring to entertain you with better detective tales than, for instance, the last one you read, *The Great Fog Robbery*."

Professor Silver brushed his hand nervously across his forehead.

"Do you mean to tell me," he exclaimed, "that none of this has happened? That Robert Chetney is not dead, that his lawyer did not find a letter of yours written from Moscow, and that just now, when he charged you with murder, he was in jest?"

"I am really very sorry," said the American, "but you see, he could not have found a letter written by me from Moscow, because I've never been to Moscow. Until this year, I've never been outside my own country. I'm not a naval officer; I'm a crime fiction writer. And tonight, when this gentleman told me that you were fond of detective stories, I thought it would be amusing to tell you one I had just mapped out this afternoon."

"But Robert Chetney is a real person," interrupted the Professor Silver, "and he did go to Africa two years ago, and he was supposed to have died, and his brother, Arthur, has been recognized as the heir. And this week he did return. I read it in the paper."

"So did I," assented the American soothingly, "and it struck me as a very good plot for a story. I mean his unexpected return from the dead, and the probable disappointment of the younger brother. So I thought that the younger brother had better murder the older one. The princess I invented out of thin air. The fog I did not have to: after last night I know all that there is to know about a Toronto fog, since I was lost in one for three hours."

Professor Silver turned grimly to the Queen's Messenger. "But this gentleman," he protested, "is not a writer of short stories; he's on the staff of the Ministry of Foreign Affairs. I have seen him in the Ottawa bridge club often, and, according to him, the Princess Jasmine is not an invention. He says she is very well known — that she tried to rob him."

The servant of the Foreign Office looked unhappily at the professor and puffed nervously at his cigar.

"It's true, Professor Silver, that I am a Queen's Messenger," he said, "and a woman once did try to rob a Queen's Messenger on a railway train — only it did not happen to me but to a colleague of mine. The only Chinese princess I ever knew called herself Anna May. She used to dance at the Peking Bar on Yonge Street."

Professor Silver, with a snort of indignation, confronted the young lawyer. "And I suppose yours was a false story too? Don't tell me," he protested, "that you are not Jarndyce's son, either."

"I'm sorry," said the youngest member, smiling with embarrassment, "but my name is not Jarndyce. I assure you, though, that I know the Jarndyce family very well and that I'm on very good terms with them."

"You should be," exclaimed the Professor, "and judging from the liberties you take with the Chetneys, you had better be on very good terms with them, too."

The young man leaned back and glanced toward the servants at the far end of the room.

"It's been so long since I've been in this club," he said, "that I doubt if even the waiters remember me. Joseph may. Joseph!" he called, and at the name, one of the waiters stepped briskly forward. The young man pointed to the silver trophy that was displayed above the fireplace.

"Joseph," he said, "Please tell these gentlemen who presented that to the club."

Joseph, unused to making speeches, shifted nervously from one foot to the other. "You — you did, sir," he stammered.

"Of course I did!" exclaimed the young man. "So tell the gentlemen who I am. They wouldn't believe me."

"Who you are, sir?" said Joseph. "You're Edam Chetney's son, Robert Chetney."

"You must admit," said Robert Chetney, when the noise had died away, "that I couldn't remain dead while my little brother was being accused of my murder. I had to do something. Family pride demanded it."

"It is time you knew, Professor," the man with the pink shirt said, "that you have been the victim of what I may call a bridge conspiracy. These stories have had a more serious purpose than merely to amuse. They've been told with the express purpose of keeping you away from the Royal York Hotel. I should tell you that all through this evening, I've had a kibitzer following the match on BBO with instructions to let me know as soon as the final quarter started. He has done so."

Professor Silver glanced keenly at the man with the pink shirt and then at his watch. The smile disappeared from his lips and his face set in stern and forbidding lines.

"And may I know," he asked icily, "what was the point of your plot?"

"Obviously," the other retorted, "my object was to keep my team from exiting the Spingold today."

Professor Silver's face bloomed with brilliant color. His body shook with suppressed emotion.

"You should spend more time playing bridge and less time plotting against your opponents!" he cried. "Whatever made you do something so unsportsmanlike and underhanded?"

"That was my fault," the American said. "I've fallen on hard times lately and when I was offered a large sum of money to delay you beyond the starting time, I succumbed to temptation and then enlisted these other two gentlemen to assist me."

"And who bribed you — this fellow here?" asked Professor Silver.

"No, sir, it was your teammates!"

Professor Silver thought that over for a few moments, then looked up and spoke.

"Well, gentlemen, you weren't as successful as you think you were. As I was listening to your story, I became suspicious of a group of strangers all becoming involved in an adventure of such complexity. I took the opportunity to text my team and inform them that I was indisposed and told them to find a substitute for me this evening. Yes, I know messaging is against the rules here, but this seemed to be an exceptional circumstance. They recruited one of the kibitzers who had already begun to gather in anticipation of my arrival. The volunteer was John Carruthers, an excellent club player who occasionally shows flashes of genius. Fortunately he didn't have much to do until he found himself declaring what turned out to be the swing hand of the match. Come closer, gentlemen, and you will be able to see the hand on my iPad — I have been following my team's progress on BBO." And he drew the small tablet out its place of concealment under his book, and showed them this layout:

Dealer North. EW vul.

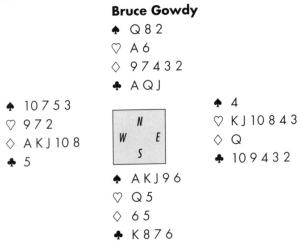

Bruce Gowdy
♠ Q 8 2
♡ A 6
◇ 9 7 4 3 2
♣ A Q J

♠ 10 7 5 3
♡ 9 7 2
◇ A K J 10 8
♣ 5

♠ 4
♡ K J 10 8 4 3
◇ Q
♣ 10 9 4 3 2

♠ A K J 9 6
♡ Q 5
◇ 6 5
♣ K 8 7 6

West	Bruce Gowdy	East	Carruthers
	1♦	2♡	2♠
3♦	3♠	pass	4♠
all pass			

"As you can see, the 4-1 trump split prohibits you from cashing your tenth trick, the fourth club. If you draw all the trumps, and then run the clubs, you can't get to your hand to cash the king. Overtaking dummy's club jack is suicide, as you promote East's ten. But our intrepid kibitzer found the answer: while he was drawing all of West's spades, he discarded dummy's ♡A.

"Now he was able to cash dummy's clubs and lead dummy's last heart toward his ♡Q. The ♡Q and the ♣K provided Tricks 9 and 10. At the other table, the same contract failed when the enemy declarer couldn't find the entry-creating play of discarding the ♡A.

"That was the turning point, and I'm afraid your team is now so far behind it's mathematically impossible for them to recover."

Professor Silver rose and bowed. "I have to thank you, gentlemen," he said, "for a most interesting evening. Among other things, it amused me to observe four apparently intelligent people swallow the preposterous notion that murder and mayhem might be committed by international spies over a copy of the rules of a card game. Perhaps one of you might be interested in buying a map showing the location of Blackbeard's buried treasure?"

Joseph had delivered the dinner bill, and now the man with the pink shirt shoved it toward the American.

"You pay it," he said.

During the last, lengthy narrative, one or two more people had checked into the hotel, which was surely full by now. The latest had apparently arrived by motorcycle. He was tattooed, clad in black leather, and wearing a red bandana. There was no evidence of a helmet in his possession. He had been listening to the end of the club member's tale as he completed the check-in process, and now he sauntered across the lounge toward our group.

"I'll tell you about a real Nationals," he said, apparently not caring whether anyone was paying attention. "It was back when people weren't cool with just whining about injustices — they did something about them. Occupy Wall Street? Bah — we occupied the Nationals! Here's how it went down…"

8

THE PROTESTER'S TALE

So the first Friday night of the tournament, this bunch of black-masked thugs marches into downtown Toronto carrying torches and Molotov cocktails. These dudes call themselves the "99% Bridge Players" in honor of Life Master truther John Carruthers, and they're putting some stiffness into the spines of the people who lost their previous stand-off with the one percent last fall in New York.

I'm going back to Hamilton, to my folks' house, and I'm packing my gear into a backpack. Their place ain't no Ritz, but compared to the marble halls where I normally work, it's all right. Big-screen in the basement, all-you-can-eat combos — what more could a bridge player want? Besides, who wants to watch his loser partner screw up hands on BBO all day? All the more reason to get out of that hellhole for the weekend and stop by the Royal York for a little anarcho-socialist action.

So I make sure my "Twelfth Brigade Occupy the Nationals" patch is clearly visible on my army field jacket and put on my Che tee-shirt that says "If you want to score at the bridge table, you've got to turn a few tricks." I don't text anyone, just jump into my Chevy Volt and head for that beast called the Summer Nationals.

You can feel the danger in the air. The blacktop roads slink ahead into the darkness like a slick, shiny snake whose raised head is poised to inject her lethal venom into the one-percenters. Driving down the QEW into the city, I'm filled with a sick anticipation that this night could be my last. I'm ready to die for my cause, man. Cold Play's "Paradise" is playing and I crank it up.

So I get to the scene, and the pigs are already there. Some kibitzers are cheering on the ninety-nine percenters, and the cops are standing there in riot gear like a bunch of dumbasses. I park my Volt in a side alley next to a bike rack, grab my hand-held mic set and digital camcorder, and run out into the wild streets. I'm thinking, tonight could be the night that YouTube makes me a star.

I'm also thinking that if there's a time to strike for the cause, it's now. Everyone in the ninety-nine percent should be willing to fight and die for equality, and I want to show that to the morons in the ACBL. Filming this experience, displaying the social injustice of the rating system, it's all footage I plan on having for when I apply to the journalism school at Ryerson.

So I rush into the fray, not giving a shit about what lies ahead. A wall of policemen stands in front of me, their backs presenting an impressive line. The anarchists face them like demigods brought down from the hills of Muskoka to draw a line in the sand. "No further shall you Grand Life Masters pass."

Now's the time to put up or shut up. I join the mob and dozens of Guy Fawkes masks greet me. I can tell they think I'm cool. I pull out my mic and start asking questions.

"So what brings you to downtown Toronto this fine evening?" I ask the first rioter I find.

"Mmmph" is all I get. I tell the man to take off his mask and the masterpoint slip taped across his mouth so we can start the interview again.

"Fucking pigs die!" the man screams in primal rage, belting out a war cry that would shame Bruce Gowdy. He whips a brick at a cop, who blocks it. A few seconds later, a tear gas canister clinks down next to me. A man in a Guy Fawkes mask grabs my arm and tells me to run. So I follow him. We run to a street corner with a Starbucks. By then I'm super thirsty — I could really go for a frappuccino right about now.

"What are your demands?" I ask one of the rioters.

"We believe in equality of outcomes, abolishing entry fees, and licence to smoke at the table," the man yells before hurling a steel ball at the Starbucks window and shattering it. He enters the building, and I follow him, mic in hand.

"We want the ACBL to pay for everything, or else nobody gets anything. They can start by paying for everybody's bridge games, beer, and parking."

"Card fees, beer, *and* parking?" I ask.

"Right! You've heard of the War on Women?" he shouts as a Molotov cocktail splashes blue flames up the coffeehouse wall.

"What?" I ask, dodging a vanilla shaker. These guys are really into it. Someone grabs a chair and starts smashing up the joint.

"The War on Women, remember?"

I nod.

"Well, we believe that all men and women should have equal access to sex, so we want ACBL financing of hookers and fifteen-minute sex breaks between rounds. Same for pot, blow, crank ... whatever floats your boat. The point is everyone gets and can do whatever he or she wants."

"Anything else?" I ask sarcastically.

"Yes, equal opportunity scoring at all ACBL events," he replied. "For example, I defended this hand yesterday. I was East." He pulled a crumpled hand record out of his pocket.

Dealer South. EW vul.

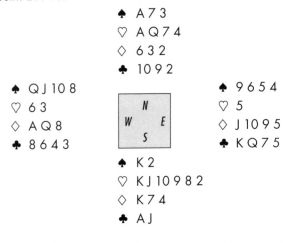

♠ A 7 3
♡ A Q 7 4
◇ 6 3 2
♣ 10 9 2

♠ Q J 10 8
♡ 6 3
◇ A Q 8
♣ 8 6 4 3

♠ 9 6 5 4
♡ 5
◇ J 10 9 5
♣ K Q 7 5

♠ K 2
♡ K J 10 9 8 2
◇ K 7 4
♣ A J

West	North	East	South
			1♡
pass	3♡	pass	4♡
all pass			

"Partner led the queen of spades and it seemed that declarer had to rely on the ace of diamonds being onside. But she saw an extra chance — that I held the king and queen of clubs. She ducked the opening lead in both hands! After winning the next spade in hand, she crossed to dummy by leading the jack of hearts to the queen and then played a small club. She took my queen with the ace, played the eight of hearts to the ace, threw her jack of clubs on the spade ace, and then led the ten of clubs. After ruffing my club king with the king, she played the two of hearts to dummy's seven and threw a diamond on the nine of clubs. Finally, she led a diamond to the king, but there was no over-trick, as my partner held the ace behind her. She lost a spade and two diamonds, making four hearts."

"Well-thought-out," I comment. "So she played the hand expertly — what's your beef?"

"You can't have experts playing in the tournament if everyone's equal. At the other table, my teammate played on clubs but East got in and played a diamond through. One down and we lost twelve IMPs. Of course, we lost the match and were eliminated."

"Okay, so the other team played better than yours and advanced to the next round…"

"Meritocratic reward is a shallow intellectual construct adopted by that happy one percent, the experts, to justify their position *vis-à-vis* the great sea of non-experts. As a theory of justice or just distribution, it's a fiction. Its source derives from the same stream of thought in which social Darwinists and efficient capitalists dip for their philosophies. As bridge continues its disturbing journey, marked by frequent defeats and humiliations, it's just as likely for the scum as for the cream to rise to the top, and not invariably because of their hard work."

Behind me a bullhorn blares. "This is the police. Come out with your hands up and lie down on the sidewalk in single file. We will not ask you twice."

"So you're an anarchist and you support all these demands for freebies?" I ask.

"We're not *not* with the Occupy movement," the guy says as he yoinks a danish off the counter. "Anyway, you can't have masterpoint rankings when everyone's equal. You ever read post-structuralism?"

Some guy on the counter starts emptying a cash register onto the floor and the rioters snatch up loose change.

"Yeah," I reply, "class hierarchy really sucks. Ever since my rich banker dad cut off my trust fund, I've been ruminating about the capitalist system of exploitation."

"Little dude, it's time to go!" he yells, making a mad rush for the back door.

From Starbucks, I manage to make my way to the hotel and the main ballroom where the knockout teams are sitting down at the tables. Then I see Rosa Luxemburg dragging a chair to the centre of the room. She hoists her bulk up on the chair and starts waving her arms at the bridge players.

"Comrades!" she shouts. "Why do you waste your time and money engaging in a contest that you're doomed to lose? It is because the one percent have conditioned you to accept an unfair arrangement as right and proper. You sit down to play and don't even notice that one percent of the players leave with eighty-five percent of the masterpoints. Only through the conscious action of the lower bridge classes can reform be brought about; only through the players' highest intellectual maturity and inexhaustible idealism can it be brought safely through all storms and find its way to port."

"Right on! Masterpoints for everyone!" one of her supporters yells. They're filling up the room right quick.

"The more that bridge democracy develops and grows and becomes stronger," Rosa goes on, "the more the enlightened masses of players will take their own destinies, the leadership of their movement, and the distribution of masterpoints into their own hands. Count the tables, calculate the masterpoints available to the match, and distribute them equally among all the players. Then proceed with the event in the secure knowledge that each will receive her fair share of masterpoints."

"No more score comparisons! Take back accumulated masterpoints and give them to the people," chanted her minions.

"Expert-class domination is undoubtedly a historical necessity, but so too is the rising of the Little Old Lady class against it. Masterpoint accumulation is also a historical necessity, but so too is its gravedigger, the bridge proletariat." Rosa bats at the three directors who are trying to get her down from the chair. "Bridge professionals out!" she hollers, catching one of the guys in the face. "Return any masterpoints from anyone holding more than two hundred to the masses and end masterpoint requirements to play in any event. Make all games open to all bridge players! Tax the masterpoint-rich players through redistribution. End entry fees!" The crowd cheers.

Then these police stormtroopers rush through the doors. It's like we're in a real war. Cops file in through the door, grab some of the protesters by the collars and zip-tie them on the ground. I'm grabbed by my ponytail and thrown on the floor, which smells weirdly like bagels and cream cheese. I plan on suing the department, man, even though I got away after the dude cuffing me was hit on the back of the head with a bottle of Molson's.

I end up going back to the hotel room I'm sharing with fifteen of my closest friends and calling it a night.

The next day is my annual game with the prof so I get to the playing room and I see this poster that says "Equal Opportunity Pairs Event." So now apparently this event's free, and there's no masterpoint restrictions or comparative scoring.

I find the prof and join him at the table.

"My treat," he says as I sit. Then along comes Rosa Luxemburg and her partner Gustav Lubeck, our first opponents.

The first hand is pretty interesting:

Dealer West. Both vul.

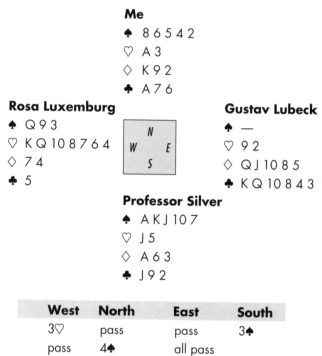

Me
- ♠ 8 6 5 4 2
- ♡ A 3
- ◇ K 9 2
- ♣ A 7 6

Rosa Luxemburg
- ♠ Q 9 3
- ♡ K Q 10 8 7 6 4
- ◇ 7 4
- ♣ 5

Gustav Lubeck
- ♠ —
- ♡ 9 2
- ◇ Q J 10 8 5
- ♣ K Q 10 8 4 3

Professor Silver
- ♠ A K J 10 7
- ♡ J 5
- ◇ A 6 3
- ♣ J 9 2

West	North	East	South
3♡	pass	pass	3♠
pass	4♠	all pass	

Prof. Silver's decision to balance at the three-level is risky, but I put down what looks to me like an excellent dummy. West leads the king of hearts and the prof wins with dummy's ace. A trump to the ace isn't so awesome: turns out West holds all three trumps. Excellent dummy or not, looks like declarer's got five losers.

The prof tells me later that he decided that his only chance was to strip West of her minor-suit cards. He knew she was holding three trumps and probably a seven-card heart suit. "So, I needed to find her with two diamonds and a singleton club," he tells me.

Anyway, so Prof. Silver draws a second round of trumps and cashes the ace and king of diamonds, followed by the ace of clubs. Next, he throws West in, exiting with the jack of hearts to the queen. She can cash the queen of trumps but then she's got to play a heart.

This gives declarer a potential ruff-and-discard, right, and he's got to be careful to discard a diamond from dummy and a club from his hand (or the other way around). West's still on lead and has to play another heart. The prof ruffs this one in dummy and tosses the last club from his hand. He then crossruffs the remaining tricks, making the contract.

Rosa totally freaks out. "Director!" she yells, but a player at the next table tells us that there's no directors available, because they were paid out of the entry fees. All we could do was take disputes to an appeal committee that would have been made up of volunteers.

So we go to this appeals committee after, and Rosa starts bitching about it being unfair that she has to defend a slam against an expert declarer. That cracks up Bruce Gowdy, who's the committee chairman.

"Expert?" He can't quit laughing. "You're calling the Professor an expert?"

"Well, he has hundreds of masterpoints," Rosa says.

"No, as of this morning, everyone has only two hundred master-points, so you have the same ranking as any other bridge player," this other committee guy tells her.

And Rosa goes, "But he also has sixty years of experience, which is far more than the rest of us. That's an advantage and very unfair."

"No," says Mr. Gowdy, "he's had one year's experience sixty times."

"Technically, she's right," one of the committee members says. And then they decide to adjust her score: average minus for me and the Professor and average plus for Rosa.

For some reason, the prof decides not to play in the evening session. As I leave the building, I go over all the shit that's happened in the last couple of days. While interviewing those brooding warriors at the class struggle's front lines, I found that radical leftists, progressives, and anarchists see eye-to-eye on the important stuff, like masterpoint inequality, equality of outcomes, and free bridge. They're so obvious to intelligent bridge players, even professionals and average players can figure them out.

Gives you hope for the future of the game, doesn't it?

EPILOGUE

The evening ended eventually, as all such evenings must, when the coffee ran dry. Our motley crew drifted away to their various bedrooms, to meet again in a faintly embarrassed way the next morning over plates of overcooked eggs and do-it-yourself waffles. Jointly and severally, we resumed our pilgrimage, the Nationals took place as always, and the results became a matter of record.

I could not help wondering how many of the stories I'd heard had any kernel of truth to them. Surely, there must have been one or two that had more or less happened as described. Indeed, at times I still wonder.

I did not know it at the time, but there was one final tale to be told, one that clearly deserved a place in our canon. I heard it some years later, this time after a bridge game. I can vouch for its authenticity, since the person who told it to me actually attended the fateful garden party that started the whole unhappy chain of events.

"You'll find your father greatly changed," Mrs. Silver remarked as she turned the car into the gates of the provincial mental hospital.

"Does he have to wear hospital clothes?" asked Cheryl.

"No, dear, of course not. He's receiving the very best attention." It was Cheryl's first visit and it was being made at her own suggestion. Months had passed since that late summer day when Professor Silver had been taken away at her mother's annual garden party, a charity event given to raise money for indigent bridge players. ("As if there were any other kind," Cheryl had remarked at the inaugural event.) The weather had been clear and brilliant with promise until the arrival of the first guests, when it had suddenly blackened into a squall. There had been a scuttle for cover, a frantic carrying of cushions and chairs, a tablecloth lofted to the branches of the maple tree, fluttering in the rain. Then a bright period and the cautious emergence of guests onto the soggy lawn, another squall, another twenty minutes of sunshine. It had been an abominable afternoon, culminating at about six o'clock in her father's attempted suicide.

Professor Silver habitually threatened suicide on the occasion of a garden party; but that year he had been found black in the face, hanging by his belt in the maple tree. Some neighbors, who were sheltering there from the rain, set him on his feet again, and before dinner an ambulance had called for him. Since then, Mrs. Silver had paid regular calls at the hospital and returned rather reticent about her experience.

Many of her relatives were inclined to be critical of Professor Silver's accommodation. He was not, of course, an ordinary inmate. He lived in a separate wing of the facility, especially devoted to the segregation of prominent persons suffering from mental illness. These were given every consideration their foibles permitted. They could choose their own clothes (many indulged in the liveliest fancies), smoke the most expensive cigars, and on the anniversaries of their admission invite any other inmates to private dinner parties. The professor was even allowed to visit the bridge club in the village from time to time.

The fact remained, however, that it was far from being the most expensive kind of institution. The uncompromising address "Provincial Care Center for Mental Illness" stamped across the notepaper, worn on the uniforms of their attendants, engraved, even, on a prominent plaque at the main entrance, suggested otherwise. From time to time, with less or more tact, Mrs. Silver's friends attempted to bring to her notice particulars of lakeside nursing homes, of "qualified practitioners with large private grounds suitable for the charge of nervous or difficult cases," but she paid no attention. When her son finally graduated from law school, he could make any changes that he thought fit; meanwhile, she felt no inclination to relax her economical regime. Her husband had betrayed her basely on the one day in the year when she looked for loyal support, and was far better off than he deserved.

A few lonely figures in overcoats shuffled about the park as Mrs. Silver and Cheryl made their way up the long driveway. They drove past the blank yellow-brick facade to the doctor's private entrance and were received by him in the Visitors Room, set aside for interviews. The window was protected on the inside by bars and wire netting; there was no fireplace. When Cheryl nervously attempted to move her chair away from the radiator, she found that it was screwed to the floor.

"Professor Silver is ready to see you," said the doctor.

"How is he?"

"Oh, very well, I'm glad to say. He had a nasty cold a while ago, but apart from that, his condition is excellent. He spends a lot of his time writing."

They heard a shuffling, skipping sound approaching along the flagged passage. Outside the door, a high peevish voice, which Cheryl recognized as her father's, said, "I haven't the time, I tell you. Let them come back later."

A gentler tone replied, "Now come along and say hello at least. They've come all this way. You don't have to stay any longer than you want to."

Then the door was pushed open (it had no lock or fastening) and Professor Silver came into the room. He was attended by a tall, elderly man with a full head of white hair and a kind expression.

"This is Mr. Gowdy — he acts as Professor Silver's attendant," the doctor said quietly to the two women.

"But I know him," said Mrs. Silver with surprise.

"Administrative assistant," corrected Professor Silver, whose hearing was apparently unaffected by whatever mental distress had overtaken him. He moved with a jogging gait and shook hands with his wife.

"This is Cheryl," said Mrs. Silver. "You remember Cheryl, don't you?"

"No, I can't say that I do. What does she want?"

"We just came to see you."

"Well, you have come at an exceedingly inconvenient time. I am very busy. Have you typed out that letter to *The Encyclopedia of Bridge* yet, Gowdy?"

"No, Professor. If you remember, you asked me to look up the probabilities of a seven-zero trump split first?"

"So I did. Well, that's fortunate, as I think the whole letter will have to be redrafted. A great deal of new information has come to light since lunch. A great deal ... You see, my dear, I am fully occupied." He turned his restless, quizzical eyes upon Cheryl. "I suppose you have come about the manuscript. Well, you must come again in a few weeks. Tell Ray he'll have it soon, but I have not had time to give my full attention to it. Tell him that."

"Very well, Dad," replied Cheryl, in an attempt to humor him.

"Anyway," said Professor Silver petulantly, "it is a matter of secondary importance. There is the *Encyclopedia* and the *Playboy* article to be dealt with first, eh, Bruce? Manuscript indeed. Nasty project, just a nuisance really. Well, can't waste any more time, nice of you to come. I would help you if I could, but you see how I'm fixed. Write to me about it. That's it. Put it in black and white." And with that he left the room.

"You see," said the doctor, "he's in excellent condition — putting on weight, eating and sleeping excellently. In fact, the tone of his system is above reproach."

The door opened again and Mr. Gowdy returned.

"Sorry to come back, sir, but I was afraid that the young lady might be upset at the Professor's not knowing her. Don't mind him, Ms. Silver. Next time he'll be pleased to see you. It's only that he's upset because he's behind with his work. All this week I've been helping out in the library and so I haven't been able to get all his notes typed out. And he's got muddled with his card index. That's all it is. He doesn't mean harm."

"What a nice man," said Cheryl, when Mr. Gowdy had gone back to his charge.

"Yes. I don't know what we'd do without old Gowdy."

"Everybody loves him, staff and patients alike."

"I remember him from years ago — he was a bridge player too. It's a great comfort to know that you're able to get such good attendants," said Mrs. Silver. "People who don't know say such foolish things about places like this."

"Oh, but Bruce isn't an attendant," said the doctor.

"You don't mean he's crazy too?" said Cheryl.

The doctor corrected her. "He's a patient — rather an interesting case, actually. He's been here for thirty-five years."

"But he seems completely sane," said Cheryl.

"He certainly has that air," said the doctor, "and for the last twenty years, we've treated him as such. He's the life and soul of the place. He's not one of the private patients, but we allow him to mix freely with them. He plays bridge excellently, does conjuring tricks at our annual concert, helps them with their crossword puzzles and various — er — hobbies. We allow them to give him small tips for services rendered; by now he's probably amassed a small fortune. He has a way with even the most troublesome of them. An invaluable man about the place."

"Yes, but why is he here?"

"Well, it is rather sad. When he was a young man, he got into a furious argument with another player over a bridge hand. It ended in a fist fight outside the bridge club, and the other fellow fell and hit his head on something and later died. Bruce has been here ever since."

"It must have been some comment!" observed Cheryl.

"It was!" he replied. "I know the hand in question, because we've discussed it many times in his therapy sessions. Bruce was playing 4♠ against a brash young rookie on this layout early in the evening.

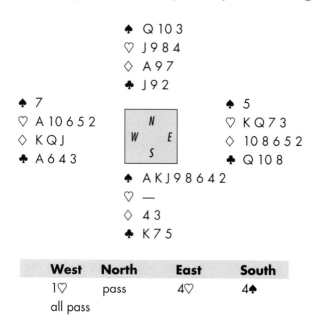

	♠ Q 10 3	
	♡ J 9 8 4	
	◇ A 9 7	
	♣ J 9 2	
♠ 7		♠ 5
♡ A 10 6 5 2	N	♡ K Q 7 3
◇ K Q J	W E	◇ 10 8 6 5 2
♣ A 6 4 3	S	♣ Q 10 8
	♠ A K J 9 8 6 4 2	
	♡ —	
	◇ 4 3	
	♣ K 7 5	

West	North	East	South
1♡	pass	4♡	4♠
all pass			

"The diamond king was led, and Bruce won with the ace, East signaling an odd number of diamonds — which, after the first trump, suggested that West started with 1=5=3=4 shape. Realizing that the club ace was likely to be on his left, Bruce drew a round of trumps and played a club, ducking in both hands. The defense cashed a diamond and West played the heart ace. Bruce ruffed and played a low club toward the dummy, obviously hoping for a doubleton ace to appear. But East won with the queen and returned the suit to his partner's ace. One down, losing three clubs and a diamond.

"'I guess one gets too old to play bridge,' said the rookie fatefully. 'A little thought would have revealed the winning line of play. You need to use your trump entries to ruff hearts in hand. Basically, you strip the hand and endplay one of us in diamonds to break clubs for you. It's a little complex, with a few variations, but I'm sure you can work it out later if you look at the hand records.'

"In those days, Bruce was infamous for his short fuse, and some kind of altercation was inevitable. Sadly, this one had a tragic ending."

"But if you believe he's perfectly harmless now, why has he not been released?"

"Well, I suppose if anyone were interested, he would be. He has no relatives except a stepsister who lives in Victoria. She used to visit him at one time, but she hasn't been for years now. He's perfectly happy here and I can assure you we aren't going to turn him out. He's far too useful to us."

"But it doesn't seem fair," said Cheryl.

"Look at your father," said the doctor. "He'd be quite lost without Gowdy to act as his admin."

. . .

Cheryl left the institute oppressed by a sense of injustice.

"It still doesn't seem fair. Think of being locked up in a loony bin all one's life."

Her mother was unsympathetic. "He attempted to hang himself at my garden party," she replied, "in front of all those Life Masters."

"I don't mean Dad. I mean Mr. Gowdy."

"A very decent man, I thought, and eminently suited to his work here."

Cheryl left the question for the time, but returned to it again the following day.

"Mom, what does one have to do to get people out of that mental hospital?"

"The hospital? Good gracious, I hope that you don't want your father to be let out!"

"No, no — Mr. Gowdy."

"Cheryl, this is all very odd. I see it was a mistake to take you with me on our little visit yesterday."

Cheryl disappeared to her room and was soon immersed in researching her new interest on Wikipedia. She did not reopen the subject with her mother, but a few weeks later when there was a question of taking some bagels over to her father for his Admission Party she showed an unusual willingness to run over with them. Her mother was occupied with other things and noticed nothing suspicious.

Cheryl drove her small car to the institution, and after delivering the bagels, asked for Mr. Gowdy. He was busy at the time making a crown for a patient who expected hourly to become Emperor of Brazil, but he left his work and enjoyed several minutes' conversation with her. They spoke about her father's health and spirits.

After a time, Cheryl remarked, "Don't you ever want to get away?"

Mr. Gowdy looked at her with his gentle blue-grey eyes. "I've got used to the life, Ms. Silver. I'm fond of the people here, and I think that several of them are quite fond of me. At least, I think they would miss me if I were to go."

"But don't you ever think of being free again?"

"Oh yes, of course I think of it — almost all the time."

"What would you do if you got out? There must be *something* you would rather do than stay here."

The old man fidgeted uneasily. "Well, I can't deny I would welcome a little outing, perhaps just once, before I get too old to enjoy it. I expect we all have our secret ambitions, and there *is* one thing I often wish I could do. Don't ask what... It wouldn't take long. But I do feel that if I did it, then I would die in peace. I could settle down again easier, and devote myself to the poor folks here with a better heart."

There were tears in Cheryl's eyes that afternoon as she drove away.

"He *will* have his little outing," she said.

From that day onwards for many weeks, Cheryl had a new purpose in life. She moved about the ordinary routine of her home with an abstracted air and an unfamiliar, reserved courtesy that greatly disconcerted her mother.

I believe the child's in love, thought Mrs. Silver. *I only pray that it isn't that rude Epstein boy.*

Cheryl read a great deal on the Internet. She quizzed her brother, she cross-examined any guests who had pretensions to legal or medical knowledge, and she wrote to old Roderick Foscote, their federal MP. The names "psychiatrist," "lawyer," and "government official" now had for her the glamor that formerly surrounded film actors and professional bridge players. She was a woman with a cause, and before the end of the year she had triumphed. Mr. Gowdy was awarded his liberty.

The doctor at the hospital showed reluctance but no real opposition. Foscote applied to the minister of health. The necessary papers were signed, and at last the day came when Mr. Gowdy could take leave of the home where he had spent such long and useful years.

His departure was marked by some ceremony. Cheryl and Roderick Foscote sat with the doctor at the front of the main dining room. Before them were assembled every patient in the institution thought to be able to endure the excitement.

Professor Silver, with a few suitable expressions of regret, presented Mr. Gowdy with a copy of the newest edition of *Bridge the Silver Way*; those who supposed themselves to be emperors showered him with decorations and titles of honor. The staff presented him with a watch and many of the patients were in tears.

The doctor made the main speech of the afternoon.

"Remember," he urged, "that you leave behind you nothing but our warmest good wishes. If at any time in the future you should grow tired of your life in the world, there will always be a welcome for you here."

A dozen or so variously afflicted patients hopped and skipped after him down the drive until the iron gates opened and Mr. Gowdy stepped into freedom. His small suitcase had already gone to the bus station by cab; he had elected to walk. He had been reticent about his plans, but he was well provided with money, and the general impression was that he would go to Toronto and perhaps play a little bridge before visiting his stepsister in British Columbia.

Thus, everyone was surprised to see him return within two hours of his liberation. He was smiling whimsically, a gentle, self-regarding smile of reminiscence.

"I have come back," he informed the doctor. "I think that now I will be here for good."

"But, Gowdy, what a short time you've been gone. You can hardly have enjoyed yourself at all."

"Oh, I've enjoyed myself *very much*. I'd been promising myself one little treat for a while now. It was short but *most* enjoyable. Now I shall be able to settle down again to my work here without any regrets."

Half a mile up the road from the gates, they later discovered an abandoned bicycle. It was a racing machine of some antiquity. Near it in the ditch lay the strangled body of Professor Silver, who, riding to the local bridge club to join the evening duplicate game, had chanced to overtake Mr. Gowdy as he strode along, musing on his new opportunities.

STORY ORIGINS

1. *The Fellowship of the Ring* by J.R.R. Tolkien; *Outward Bound* by Sutton Vane

2. "The Landlady" by Roald Dahl

3. *The Adventures of Marco Polo*, Richard J. Walsh ed.

4. "The Secret Lover" by Peter Lovesey

5. "Mr. Bearstowe Says" by Anthony Berkeley

6. *Three Dialogues Between Hylas and Philonous* by George Berkeley

7. "In the Fog" by Richard Harding Davis

8. "Exclusive report: Occupy Movement's 'Black Bloc' anarchists Demand Government Handouts" by Kyle Becker http://www.conservativedailynews.com/2012/04/exclusive-report-occupy-movements-black-bloc-anarchists-demand-government-handouts/

9. "Mr. Loveday's Little Outing" by Evelyn Waugh

MASTER POINT PRESS ON THE INTERNET

www.masterpointpress.com

Our main site, with information about our books and software, reviews and more.

www.teachbridge.com

Our site for bridge teachers and students—free downloadable support material for our books, helpful articles, forums and more.

www.bridgeblogging.com

Read and comment on regular articles from MPP authors and other bridge notables.

www.ebooksbridge.com

Purchase downloadable electronic versions of MPP books and software.